One
Good
Man

ONE GOOD MAN

Del Staecker

ABSOLUTELY AMAZING eBOOKS

ABSOLUTELY AMAZING eBOOKS

One
Good
Man

AT THE PARTY

The heroin donned its mask of euphoric confusion to escort the young woman on a downward spiral toward oblivion. She was wasted. Gone. Damned, but did not know it. Alone on the sofa, she mumble-whispered to no one in particular, "I don't like the way I feel...don't like it...at...all."

The party swirled on around her. Young women with tight bodies, tighter clothes, and too much makeup bobbed and weaved between pairs and small groups of old well-heeled men eager for sex. She could not participate in the teasing rituals performed for the guests.

Struggling against the drug, she put up a fight, but the junk was winning. Limp, barely conscious, simultaneously here and somewhere far away, she began to fade. It was all she could do to focus upon the carbon copy of herself standing across the room. Her twin, a reflection-perfect look-alike, her best friend, her fellow traveler, the one who got her here, gave her the dose and did not know how the drug was consuming her friend's essence. Her double could not see her, could not sense the danger, nor could she offer aide.

The "old man," the host, stood in the way and blocked their eye contact. Perfectly in charge, the old man was the personification of money and power. Everything orbited around him. She was a satellite gone astray.

The young woman struggled. Tried to think, strained to remember. *Why am I here? Why are we here?*

The plan was to leave the Shore. Steal the Big Apple. Chew it up. Spit it into the faces of the small town go-a-longs that never had the guts to break free. Smart. Ruthless. Sleek. Sexy. We were going to hold the whip. We were going to be in control. We were...were...

She blacked out. No one noticed when she slumped between the cushions of the couch and stopped breathing.

When informed of her death the elderly host was nonplused. He coolly stated, "Get Raff. Have him take care of it." Smiling at no one in particular, he waved his guests toward the patio, away from where she forever slept.

The music pulsed, young women pranced, the old men leered, and no one paid the slightest attention to her being carried away. And, the party went on.

UNDER THE BOARDWALK

Starlight slipped through the gaps between the boards of the famed boardwalk to form a patchwork of light and dark below, and from within the shadows feral cats hissed at the intruder in their realm. Unfazed by the anxious animals Louis Green continued to dig a sandy grave beside the lifeless girl.

"Dammit!" he winced in pain, wiggling his fingers to ease the throbbing. Louis had undergone several chemical treatments to remove his prints. Digging in the sand irritated the scar tissue on his fingertips. "Fingers ain't never gonna heal," he muttered as he dug.

The cats edged nearer to watch and he paused to assess them.

Well-fed parasites – nothing but pampered, well-fed parasites. That's all they are.

Louis continued to work alongside the body as he estimated the number of cats.

Must be close to twenty. They shouldn't be hungry 'cause those damn animal rights freaks feed 'em all the time.

He threw a handful of sand in their direction.

What a sorry-assed world. Full of do-gooder hypocrite assholes. They care more about cats than people. Walk right past some down-and-outs to pamper a fuckin' animal that ought to fend for itself.

Known along the Jersey Shore as Rasta Man Raff, Louis was not new to gruesome tasks. As a pimp and drug-pusher in Chicago, and now in Atlantic City, he had seen plenty of women overdose. Louis disposed of them, too.

The cats came closer.

Maybe this bunch hasn't been fed.

3

Raff threw sand at the circling felines. "Can't have these pussies eatin' pussy!" He laughed at his sick joke, grabbed more sand, and threw it in the direction of the hissing.

The animals held their ground. It was their turf and he was an intruder.

Raff returned to his task, while keeping an eye on the cats.

Damn, this one is already getting ripe.

He waved the smell away from his nose and dug deeper.

A day and a half is too long a wait to cover her. But things got wild – her dying when and where she did. Right in the middle of the old man's party! Put her in my van...then the damn engine died...what a mess!

The cats tightened their circle.

He dug more.

When the hole was as deep as the others he had buried, Raff cut the clothes off the girl. He wadded them into a ball, and shoved them in a plastic trash bag. Then he snatched her necklace and earrings, placed them in a smaller bag, failing to see the bracelet on the girl's wrist.

I can get something extra for this stuff.

The cats drew closer as he rolled the girl into the hole.

Good thing I brought my stuff.

Raff reached for a plastic jug and doused the body with its contents.

Whew – this shit is strong! Hot sauce and concentrated citronella – drives 'em crazy.

He fanned the vapors toward the nearest cat. It caught a whiff, wailed wildly, and sped away. A second curious scavenger cautiously tested the air, caught a smell of the mixture, and rocketed straight up to the underside of the boardwalk. It ricocheted between the sand and the wood planks several times, and finally scampered after the first sniffer.

Raff congratulated himself. *My man, you are a genius!*

He returned to his task and began filling the hole. He did not look at the girl. "Gottta hurry, gotta hurry!" he murmured. The bloody scar tissue on his burnt fingertips ached, but he did not stop until his task was finished.

Damn pity she's dead, he thought. She OD'd before the higher-ups got a shot at her, and I was hopin' to sample some of that young sweet stuff before putting her out on the street with the others.

Raff resumed his work, completed an additional small burial, and marked the spot.

Some money for an emergency. Never know when I'll need to leave in a hurry.

When he emerged from beneath Atlantic City's famous boardwalk it was ten minutes past three in the morning. Since his arrival from Chicago and his complete transformation into the faux-islander persona, Raff had been busy. In the past year he had buried three other women under the beach resort's famed boards.

"Just like back home," he told himself. "When bodies need to disappear, I'm the man."

He climbed over the boardwalk rail and nodded to the figure standing guard staring at the dark horizon.

"Get moving," the lookout ordered. "The foot patrol is due back any minute."

"Back? You mean I been diggin' when *another cop* was up here?"

"Yeah, a couple minutes ago. He's gone, for now. I sent him on an errand."

"Errand? How'd you pull that off?"

"I flashed my gold shield. What do you think I did, chat him up about you under the boards burying a body?"

"But-"

"But nothing! I told you he's coming back. My badge bought you some time, which is almost out. Now, get moving."

"Sure, sure, I'm movin', I'm movin'. I gotta go. I got one of my girls waitin' for me in the van."

"You must be crazy! Which one of your bitches came with you? It better not be that nosy sleaze doing your recruiting?

"No – no not her. It's Glenda – I got Glenda with me."

"What happened to the sleaze?"

"She bolted because of the one under the boards. They were tight. She ran off with the boat guy who was sniffin' around like she was somethin' special." Raff's fingers ached and he wanted to go home to soak them. Frustrated, he asked, "Why are you askin' so much about her?"

"I don't like snoops. She's always asking questions – nosing around way too much. The cop in me says she had her own plans."

"I told you she's gone," affirmed Raff. "She's no worry for us." His statement had no effect on the gold shield cop.

"It's another screw up in a long line of them. You've got troubles. I told you not to play two games at once. Running girls to the casino crowd isone thing. Juicing them up at the old man's is another. Just look at the mess we've got. If I had not caught wind about what happened you'd still have her stuffed in your van."

"But I took care of it!"

"And brought a witness along!"

"Glenda's good – she'll keep quiet."

"For both your sakes, I really hope so. You've got enough to worry about when you report on all this shit you've stirred up."

"Report?"

"To the Italians...they'll be waiting for you."

"Shit! Them?"

"Yeah. Shit. And *you* are in *it!*"

"Fuck them racist Eye...tail...yens!"

"Good luck."

"They're just phony wannabes makin' believe they are the Mob."

"They may be, but they are between you...me...and the old man."

The cop scanned the boardwalk, looked out to sea again, and absentmindedly murmured, "I wonder...what that sleaze recruiter of yours knows?"

To forget about the Italians, Raff butted in. "She don't know nothin'! I keep my business separate."

"At that, you've failed miserably."

"Look, I said she don't know nothin'! She ran 'cause she was too close to the one that croaked – or she's shacked-up on a boat with that dude. Maybe she's hookin' for herself."

"She's trouble. Trust me, I know who she is and where she comes from. My old partner and I busted her when she was just a juvie."

"But she's gone. Just like I said – gone!"

"I don't like her disappearing. And, I like it less you can't tell me why."

"Like I'm supposed to care *about that*? Remember?" He pointed downward. "Remember what's fresh in the sand?"

"Agreed. The missing one is not the problem – right now. You better get moving." The cop looked out at the water again.

Raff stalled. He asked, "You got more stuff comin' in?"

His query was ignored, but he lingered on the topic. *That one I buried and her missing friend knew something! They knew about stuff comin' in – big stuff – they got the news from the party crowd and I –*

The cop broke into his thoughts. "Didn't I tell you to

7

GET MOVING?"

"Okay, okay, I hear ya. I hear 'ya. I'm outta here."

Raff tucked both bags under his arm and headed north along the water's edge. He did not look back to see how his accomplice would further handle the night patrolman.

Cops! Don't feed me any bullshit about them. And, don't be tellin' me they ain't just like the rest of us. Everyone is scrapin' to get it their way and have enough to be on top. Cops are the same as everyone else.

"MAY DAY! MAY DAY!"

Zack McCoy's head throbbed with excruciating pain. On previous occasions the migraines had provided him with foolproof warnings for impending disaster. Zack had learned not to ignore them as his personal and infallible barometer for "all hell breaking loose." However, today it was not a migraine that caused his head to almost explode. This time it was different. A tangible injury was causing the problem. He was bleeding and the Gates of Hell were hanging wide open. His beloved boat, *Summer Wind*, was sinking. Blood flowed steadily from the makeshift pressure bandage he clutched behind his ear.

He told himself, "This is not good. This is really not good. Need to fix my position."

Zack looked toward shore and saw a massive circle of light. He knew where he was.

"MAYDAY! MAYDAY! MAYDAY! This is the *Summer Wind – Summer Wind – Summer Wind* – LA 1123. We are due east of Ocean City, New Jersey – distance, is approximately one mile from shore. We need pumps, medical assistance, and a sea tow –"

Zack paused, delicately patted his head, looked at the unconscious girl on the salon floor, and continued the call for help, "– one adult is on board – head injury and bleeding – estimate that *Summer Wind* can stay afloat less than one hour – *Summer Wind* is thirty-six foot vessel, white hull and white fly bridge, running lights do not function – emergency lights are on battery power – Over."

Zack repeated the message a second time in a weakened voice. Before he could begin the third attempt, he heard a reply." *Summer Wind,* this is Coast Guard Helo six-one-seven. We are airborne and en route. Can you

9

state your position? Over."

"I'm due east of the Ocean City ferris wheel. I estimate one mile. I can easily see its lights. Over."

"You should have bought that emergency positioning beacon," he scolded himself.

The Coast Guard asked, "*Summer Wind,* update your vessel's condition – over."

"Roger – wait one."

Zack stepped down into the galley and popped the hatch leading to the engine compartment. Seawater sloshed halfway up the sides of the silenced Lehman diesels.

It's worse than I thought.

Zack quickly retraced his steps and informed the Coastie helo in a shaky voice, "I am taking on water fast – my estimate for staying afloat is fifteen minutes – maximum – over."

"*Summer Wind,* this is Coast Guard Helo six-one-seven. Update your medical condition – over."

Zack ignored the call and attempted to revive his companion with smelling salts from the emergency kit. "Come on, Baby. You got to get up," he told her.

The girl's blue-green eyes flashed, she sat up, and she asked, "W – w – what the hell happened?"

"A big wave hit us."

"Are we sinking?"

"Yes," he calmly told her.

She stared into his eyes.

"We're taking on water," he added.

"How bad is it?"

He could not lie. "Real bad. But the Coast Guard is coming. We're just off Ocean City. I think you should take the raft and head there."

"What!?" She shook her head.

"Think!" he said. Staring into her beautiful eyes,

McCoy urged, "You don't want to be here. You can't be here. Understand?"

She looked down. Weakly she answered, "Okay."

He pushed her toward the deck.

In a few minutes she was over the side and headed to the beach. As the raft moved away from the boat and disappeared in the night McCoy mumbled, "It's the only way, the only way." Then he collapsed on the deck.

On the bridge, the radio squawked. "*Summer Wind,* this is Helo six-one-seven. Do you copy? Over."

There was no reply.

"*Summer Wind,* this is Helo six-one-seven. *Do you copy?* Over."

Again, there was no reply.

THE MUSIC MAN

The caller's voice was strained and serious. "This is how I see it, Joe. People don't give a damn about Jersey Shore music anymore. In fact, nobody really gives a damn about anything anymore – except the crap they see on TV."

The man with the one-of-a-kind whisky-voice replied, "Whoa, my pal, don't give yourself a big ol' case of the boardwalk blues. You are wrong, wrong, wrong. Now, listen to me. I give a damn, a big damn, and if you stop to think a minute...so...do...you. Listen – you called me to complain and I'm listening. That proves that at least the two of us care."

The caller sighed and agreed, "Yeah, Joe, yeah. I guess you're right."

"Guess? There's no guessing in it. You know I'm right. I believe in the music and so do you. For people like you the shore is not just the drunken antics of brainless louts – it's the whole package. You want the sun, sand, sea, *and* the sounds – and by that I mean the Jersey Shore Sound."

"Yeah, yeah, you're right, Joe."

"You bet I am. By the way – what's your name? Tell me, so I know who in the choir I'm preaching to."

"Jeff. My name is Jeff."

"Jeff, my friend, guys like you and me – we know the good stuff never dies. Doo Wop, rock, reggae, soul, R&B, even garage bands. If it's real it lasts.

"Are you sure?"

"Yes – definitely. In life and in music, the good stuff lives forever. That's why I do what I do. It's why I'm here, and that's why I *am* Jersey Shore Joe *the* Guardian of the Shore's Music! Ya gotta keep believing. Hang in there. Something good will happen when you least expect it. Or, maybe you'll make it happen."

"Me?"

"Yes – why not? A good man can do a lot of wonderful things."

"Like what?"

"Like helping others, doing some real good. A good man could determine his own fate and then the fate of others."

"What about someone that isn't so good? You know – a guy that's made some mistakes."

"Nobody is perfect, Jeff, and anyone can start over. Trust me."

"If you say so, Joe."

"I do. I do say so – because I know. One man's actions can change everything. Especially if he's sincere, and especially if he's a decent guy."

"Really? Do you *really* think so?

"I *know* so."

"I believe you...Thanks, Joe, thanks!"

"And, thank you for your call, Jeff." Joe paused briefly and then added his trademark phrase, "I'll catch you later...down on the shore!"

Joseph Kontos, known to all as Jersey Shore Joe, eyed the doorway to the broadcast booth, frowned, and waved for the person standing at the doorway to enter the broadcast booth.

A slight-built twenty-something male handed him a sheet of paper while Joe kept his on-air-banter going.

"Hey, all you *real* people out there on the shore! It's time to share the love and share the music. You know...the music that kills them old Jersey Shore blues, and for all you music freaks – you *know* this is where you can hear the music that will last forever! And speaking of forever, I'll be back in a moment with Little Steven and the Disciples of Soul doing *Forever*. But first, the radio-station-suits are forcing me to break away from serving you with music for an *important* message."

Joe scanned the sheet of paper. His face formed a frown as he flipped off his mike and played the next song instead of reading the offering. To the bearer of the note he said, "Wendell, this sucks, man, does it ever suck. It's always the same old crap: sick news and one uninspired ad after another." He crumpled the paper and tossed it in the waste can. "There you go, filed just where a lousy piece of crap belongs."

"Come on, Joe, stop it." Wendell said, as he retrieved the paper. "Look!" he said, pointing at the lead story on the wire service. "Right here in Atlantic City several young women are missing. Now, that's important!"

"Okay, I'll bend on that, but look at this ad. Pet grooming? At 4 a.m.? Who on earth is listening to ads for pet grooming at 4 a.m.?"

"So what if it does suck? An ad is an ad. Count yourself lucky that anyone advertises on a pathetic oldies show at 4 a.m." He smoothed out the wad of paper.

"How many times as the station's Assistant Manager do I have to suggest that you try a new format? You need to get into this century, be contemporary and play the sounds of today. *And*, the term is '*Dude* or '*Bro*.' Only an old fart would call somebody, 'Pal.'"

Joe's face soured. "There was a time when everyone loved this music, it meant something, and it's *Mister* Jersey Shore Joe to you, *Wendy*."

"The name is Wendell. Wendell Pinkering, *Junior*. You know, the same as in the name of *the station owner* Wendell Pinkering, *Senior,* my father. He's not someone you want to disappoint by making fun of his namesake."

"Speaking of disappointments – how does your Daddy feel about you? Damn-it, boy, what kind of handle is Wendell, Junior? You ever think about changing it to something more manly? You'd do much better in this world as Bart, or Jed, or something ballsy and tough. Wendell, Junior sounds like you do floral arrangements and hang out in truck-stop restrooms."

Wendell dropped the paper in front of Joe and left, saying, "That's so lame, so fucking lame. You're nothing but a washed-up-no-talent bar-singer-without-a-band turned DJ, and you're a hopeless homophobe!"

"Oh my," Joe quipped, "let's not get personal, *Pal.*" He picked up the ad copy and added, "You're the one who's got the girly name."

From outside the booth Joe heard, "Wait 'til my father hears what you said about *his name.*"

"I just call 'em the way I see 'em, *Wendy!*"

Wendell lost it and screamed back, "You sorry-ass has-been!" He pointed at the paper. "Just read what I give you or this will be your last show!"

In his distinctive voice Joe calmly replied, "I'm too old to be threatened," and stepped to the door and flipped the lock.

Jersey Shore Joe, the aging legend and self-proclaimed guardian of the Jersey Shore Sound, came back to the console and slid a well-worn cassette into the console, and Muddy Waters launched into his legendary banned tune *Champagne and Reefer*. It gave Joe time to think.

Wendell Junior is a good kid. I'd stop harassing him if he wasn't so in-my-face about things. I don't dislike anyone, or their lifestyle. I just hate being forced to choose sides about stuff I just don't care about. I say, 'Live and let live." Shore music, the sound described as, "beer, sweat, and after-shave, chasing perfume" that's my life. I must admit, ribbing him is a waste of time and energy. There's better game.

A wide smile decorated his face as Muddy Waters

finished the tune.

Our absentee leader, Wendell Senior should have listened to my advice when I wrote that equipment memo. He should have upgraded the hardware when I suggested. He'll shit a brick when he hears from the FCC about this.

Joe inserted another tape and flicked the override switch. Southside Johnny and the Asbury Jukes filled the room as Joe walked to the window and pulled out a particularly bad smelling cigar.

I've been saving this for such an occasion. I hope it sets off the fire alarm.

He lit the cigar and looked out at the night as a Coast Guard helicopter sped above Atlantic City's casinos. Joe puffed his smoke and stared at the helicopter's disappearing lights. A familiar uneasiness wrapped around him with the smoke. "I need a change, a real change," he - half-mumbled, half-prayed as he ignored the persistent pounding on the door and continued puffing, and savoring the lyrics of the song. Southside Johnny was explaining why he did not want to go home.

What's wrong with this sad-assed world is that people have forgotten how to sing. All we've got today is monotonous whining and yelling by spoiled kids with tattoos and thugs wearing gold chains.

He sighed heavily and puffed again on his cigar.

Hell, I've been tossed out of much better joints than this. Maybe, Southside Johnny is wrong. It's time for me to go home-I just have to figure where that is.

When the song's last note played Joe turned on the microphone and in his raspy voice signed off without using his trademark phrase. "This is Jersey Shore Joe simply saying goodnight, and goodbye, my friends." After one final puff Joe collected his music cassettes and carefully placed them into a satchel he called his "treasure box of musical memories." As he unlocked the door he waved for an exasperated Wendell to step aside.

"It's over – I quit. This dinosaur is headed to the bone-yard on his own."

Wendell protested, "You – you – you just can't walk out. It's 4 a.m.!"

"I know. Remember – I serve the insomniacs needing their pets groomed."

"Stop, just stop! I'm warning you. You'll pay for this!"

Joe leaned forward. "I told you *not* to threaten me, *Wendy.*" He leaned some more.

The frightened man-boy merged with the paint on the wall. Joe rasped, "And, you should stay away from those truck stops, too."

Wendell reacted with an unaccustomed intensity, "You arrogant old bastard! You'll never work in this business again. Do you understand? *If you walk out, you're finished!*" He stopped his rant when Joe addressed him once more.

Spitting his cigar to the floor, Joe stubbed out the butt's glow with a toe, and said, "Kid, I hear you making noise, but no message is coming through. Me and my music are out of here."

"Wha – wha – what!?"

"Like I just told the folks, it's goodbye."

Joe made his way to the rear exit, opened the door, and stepped into the fresh air of the Jersey Shore night. *God! It feels so good out here.* He told himself. *Why have I lived indoors?* The music he played within walled spaces and his love of the shore slammed together in Joe's heart. He ached deep inside.

I need to get away from the music business. All it has ever done is to pull me into radio stations, bars, and recording studios. I need the beach and the boardwalk. I need sun, sand, salt, and surf as much as anyone. I need a change. I think I'll get a camper, maybe a boat. Crap! I've got to get away.

Joe sniffed the air and sighed. He had no idea where he was going, or what he would do. He just felt good in making a choice not to do the same things again.

Joe, follow your own advice and go down the shore, for real.

On his way to the parking lot Joe felt a pang of guilt. Countless years of music rang in his ears as a siren call to return. Joe fought it. By the time he reached his parked truck, it had partially won. At the truck, he opened the glove box, extracted an old cassette tape and headed back to the station.

I gotta make this right.

Joe waved at a surprised Will, the night security guard, at the station's front door. Will let him in. Without making small talk, Joe marched into the control room to interrupt Wendell, Junior's meltdown by extending his hand holding the tape. "Here," was all he said.

In a reflex act, Wendell took the item. "What's this?" he almost whispered.

"Enough material to cover my exit."

"Huh? I don't understand...you...quit."

Joe shifted his weight from one leg to another. "Yes, I did."

"But...." Wendell assessed Joe's stance. "Okay. We'll pay...send a check."

There was a short silence long enough to cover the decades Joe had devoted to music. He finally said, "Forget the money. Put it to some good use...a charity or something."

With that said, Joe walked away from his life.

THE NOT SO WISE GUYS

When Anthony "Just Tony" Carapelli was upset he used the F word, a lot. In fact, his use was record setting, over-the-top, and disgusting. When coupled with his racist attitude he was an insufferable pig.

"Fuck! This is not very...fuckin'...good. Fuck! Fuck! Fuck!" he spat, not said, at his target in his best imitation of a TV tough guy. "You been fuckin' up way too fuckin' often, my fucked-up little friend."

For emphasis he poked at the plastic bag with the toe of his alligator-leather slip-on.

"Yes, you fuckin' phony Rasta fuckin' freak, you have been fuckin' up *much* too fuckin' often.

Things are a fuckin' mess, girls are fuckin' dying, and our fuckin' product is missing!" He pointed again with his shoe. This time it was in the direction of his ever-present sidekick, "Lover Boy" Joey Valentine, his partner in crime and abuse. Their well-known racism exceed all bounds and had entered into the realm of sadism.

"I was telling Joey here, just a fuckin' few minutes ago, how fuckin' upset I get when you fuck up, nigger!"

Raff bucked up at the racial slur. "Don't call me that! I'll —"

Lover Boy Joey pounced before Raff could finish. Although Joey's girth had spawned the behind-his-back nickname of "Fat Boy," he moved much quicker than expected.

With beefy hands around Raff's neck Valentine mimicked Tony, "Shut the fuck up, *Boy*! We can call you whatever we want. How about coon? You watermelon eatin' chicken fryin' spear-chuckin' eggplant! I ought to waste you for just mouthing off to my friend Tony!" He squeezed until the smaller man's eyes bugged.

"Joey, Joey, take it easy!" Just Tony ordered. "Sure, he's a lousy smart-mouthed fuck- up, but right now, he's too important to kill."

Raff's look was a plea for mercy. Lover Boy eased his grip. "Yeah, he owes us. He owes us for the dope and another couple of girls," affirmed the big man.

"One – just one – one girl – that's all," wheezed Raff. Both men laughed at his out-of-breath delivery.

Just Tony explained the facts. "No, you stinkin' little piece of shit, it's two. You owe one to replace the girl that OD'd and one more, just to make us happy. One and one is two. Do you understand?" He motioned for Lover Boy to squeeze again, which he did.

Raff's eyes almost popped.

"The man asked you a question. You got an answer?" Lover Boy asked. He stopped squeezing just enough to allow for air to enter his lungs.

Raff weakly squeaked out a reply. Yeah...sure... I...understand."

"Good!" Just Tony said. He motioned again to Lover Boy, the big man let go. Raff dropped to the floor.

"Joey, make certain he *really* understands," instructed Tony with a wiggle of his foot.

"My pleasure, Tony," Lover Boy answered as he directed a powerful kick to Raff's groin.

Raff doubled up. Joey leaned into the bent over Raff and hissed in his victim's face, "That's so you don't ever think about sampling the merchandise again before you deliver it, *Boy!*" He grabbed a handful of dreadlocks, slammed Raff's head to the floor, and delivered another kick. Joey hissed more. "Listen up. I want one of the girls to be a special order. I want blond, blue eyed, slim, and *very, very fresh*. I don't care how young she is – just get me one that hasn't been popped. No sampling, not even one touch by you. You got that, delivery *Boy*?"

He kicked his prey a third time. Raff lay still and moaned.

Just Tony laughed and interrupted his friend with instructions, "Joey, Joey, Joey! How many times do I have to explain it? Give the guy a chance to answer before you kick him again. Ya gotta wait a little. *Then*, if you don't like the answer go ahead and kick. But first, you've got to wait a little." He landed his own kick.

Lover Boy Joey laughed along with the joked instructions. "Okay, Tony, I see. I get it. I been getting ahead of myself. I guess I'm too much into my work." He leaned over and spoke to the moaning and groaning Raff. "Sorry, *Boy!* I'll slow down some and give you a chance to think about how you are going to agree with me."

The moaning continued.

Joey grabbed Raff's dreads again, lifted him to his feet, and shoved him on to a chair. "I'm taking a break, asshole. You're wearing me out." He grinned as he pulled out a cigarette pack and lighter. "Be good, or I'll re-toast your pinkies."

Just Tony pointed with his foot at the plastic bag and continued the exchange with Raff. "What's in the bag?"

Raff answered in a very weak voice. "Clothes – the girl's clothes. I – I –"

Tony went ballistic. "*Are you fuckin' crazy*? You should have ditched them *before* you fuckin' came to see us! You fuck up as easy as you breathe!"

"I'm – I'm sorry – I –"

"You're fuckin' stupid is what you are. And, you are in deep shit." Just Tony pointed to the smaller bag. "And, genius, what the fuck's in this one?"

"A wallet...and...and...and some jewelry."

"Fuck!" screamed Just Tony. "Have you been eating dumb-ass for breakfast?" He did not wait for an answer.

"Our friends in Chicago vouched for you. He said you were experienced and reliable. At the start you were okay, but you've been nothin' but a fuck up the past couple of weeks. We had such hopes for you. Didn't we?" He looked to his partner for confirmation.

"Yeah, Tony, we had hopes," Lover Boy added. "We are always in need of good people."

Just Tony continued. "Joey and I took you in because you impressed us with your make over. Hell, you burning off your fingerprints took balls – real balls. Growing that mop, dropping all the weight, all that stuff you did to change your look was smart, real smart. Even your Momma would have trouble recognizing you now. So, I ask. Why all the bonehead moves recently?"

There was no reply.

"I'll tell you what I think. I think you been using product, that's what."

"No, man – no, I –"

"Shut the fuck up! Don't even try denying it. I know everything. One of your street girls, Francine, she ratted you out."

"Women, can't trust 'em," commented Lover Boy Joey. "I bet she aced that new girl. Maybe she spiked the dope. Francine is just a jealous backstabbing bitch, that's what she is. I'll bet she drove off that recruiter gal you had workin' for ya, too."

"You know what that means, Rasta Boy?" Just Tony said, as he opened the second bag.

"No," Raff shuddered and winced, "No – I got no idea."

"It means you that now gotta find *three* girls; two for us, and a new one for you." Just Tony pointed to the plastic bags. "While Joey and me get rid of this stuff, you convert Francine into a piece of dead meat. Any bitch who'll rat you out will rat on us. We can't have any of that."

"She doesn't know anything!" exclaimed Raff. "The only one who knows *anything* about my business is Glenda. She's the only one I can tell any stuff to, and it's only when I need a second set of hands. But Francine is okay, too."

"'Fraid not, *boy!*" Just Tony said. "Francine has been talking. I told you we can't have that! Right Joey?"

"That's right, Ton. She's a liability. We can't have no big-mouth, back-stabbing bitch anywhere near our business."

Just Tony examined the jewelry. "This is expensive stuff – real class here. I can see why you took it." He fingered the three gold and bejeweled mermaids made as earrings and a matching pendant. "You wasn't goin' to hold this back – was you?"

"No – no! I was goin' to dump it."

"Just Tony tossed the jewelry to Lover Boy. "Get rid of this. Fence it out of town." To Raff he said, "So why you still here? I want your girlfriend gone. *Pronto!* Sooner than pronto would be better!"

Very slowly Raff got up from the chair. He eyed Joey, to make certain another kick was not coming. Joey puffed on a cigarette, smiled, and waved. "Bye, bye-*Boy!*"

Raff stumbled out the door.

Just Tony gave the plastic bags to his partner and said, "Joey, after you take care of this, take care of that." Pointing to Raff, he said, "– and make sure he does as he's told."

"Sure thing, Ton."

"I mean you take care of him *personally*. As soon as you're certain that bitch of his is dead – you make Jerk Chicken out of Rasta Boy."

"Sure, Ton. I'll give the stuff to Cousin Lil in Ocean City. She has the perfect place to sell it. I'll burn the clothes myself and be back in a jiffy to check up on the eggplant. As soon as I see proof Francine has been done I'll take care of that nigger." He paused for a shrug and added, "But, don't you think maybe we should wait until after he recruits some fresh pussy?"

"It's your call, Joey. Runnin' pussy out of the casinos is steady cash – but lately the cops are hyper 'cause Rasta Boy has been careless. He's pushin' dopers out there. Users are okay but he's peddling zombies. That OD is a prime example."

"Stupid is what he is. Imagine – he's been tappin' into the pussy, using dope, and thought we'd never find out. Like the shore ain't a place where word gets around and people tell us about the things they know."

"On second thought, Joey – have one of our cop friends take care of this. Rasta Boy is too *visible* for us to be associated with him *disappearing*." He laughed at his weak attempt at a joke.

Joey chuckled. "Sure, Ton, sure – I get it – *visible* then *disappearing*. That's a good one." "For all the money we pay to have cops with us, we ought to get some actual work out of them. It's your call on who does the work – the old one or our new little pal. But make sure we are rid of any and all liabilities."

"Meaning?"

"Meaning – after Rasta Boy gets rid of Francine, get a cop to do Rasta Boy and then Glenda, too – and anyone else in the know. Like you said, on the Shore – people know."

SEMI-RETIRED

Over the phone Joe asked, "Is this Delilah Brothers Marina?"

"Yep, you found it. I'm, Bud Delilah, the owner. My brother is retired."

"I heard you had a recent wreck for sale – cheap."

"I have several. Which one you did you hear of?"

"A sport fisher – pulled in by the Coast Guard off of Ocean City."

"Yes, McCoy's old wooden one. He didn't make it, the poor bastard."

"I heard – actually saw the helo go out."

"They were too late. He died out from a knock on the head."

"That's a shame."

"Yeah, real shame. But from what I know, McCoy was due."

"Due?"

"He did more runnin' after adventure than fish – had a real taste for the fast life. For all the long distance add-ons and toys that McCoy put on that old rig he never made much money fishing. God only knows what he was really up to. Like I said – He was more into young girls than fishin'. At least that's my call."

"Is the boat now your call?"

"Yes, we're handling its disposition for his family."

"By auction?

No, no auction. Gonna sell it – priced to go fast – real fast. Motivated sellers you might say. His people need the money bad."

"I'm sorry for the family, but I suppose that's a good thing for me to hear. I'm interested.

"Come take a look."

"Exactly where are you located, Bud?"

"Northwest side of the south causeway going over to Ocean City."

"I can be there in an hour. That okay?"

"Fine, but be prepared for seeing a mess. It needs work – that's also why there's no auction scheduled. It's not very presentable."

"Not a problem, I'm looking for a project."

"That she is, that she is...ah... Mister?"

"Kontos – Joe Kontos."

"Joe Kontos? Any connection to Jersey Shore Joe Kontos?"

"I've been called that."

"Well I'll be. Jersey Shore Joe! I don't believe it. Can't wait to meet you – listened to you all the time. Even saw you perform – that was a ways back."

"That's good to know, Bud. Will you being a fan help with the price?"

Bud laughed. "No, Joe, I'm afraid I can't do anything for you there. Like I said, the McCoy family really needs the cash. It's priced as low as it can be to go fast.

"Can't blame me for trying."

"I know, I know. Tell you what, I will do you a good turn on any work done in the yard.

"Super!"

"But, remember the boat's in rough shape, took a mean hit from a rogue wave. Still interested?"

"Like I said, I'm looking for something to do."

"You taking a break from music?"

"Yes, a complete one. I'm retired."

"No! Say it ain't so!"

"I'm afraid it's true."

"What the hell happened?"

"I don't know – I really don't know. Maybe the world

moved on and I didn't."

"Well...come see me. A boat can be a wonderful fix for whatever ails a man."

"That's exactly why I called. I'll see you soon."

"Gotcha. I look forward to seein' you, 'bye, Joe."

COPS

Detective Perry Vale checked his watch for the third time in less than a minute. *Something is wrong, very wrong. She's late,* he thought. He checked his watch again, and said aloud, "She's way overdue. Should have been here by now."

Vale's partner, veteran officer Johnny Klepp, replied, "Trouble with you new guys is that you think the scum walking around out here are regular people."

"Meaning, what?"

"It's simple, Rookie, she's a skank, and she is gonna be late 'cause it's her nature."

"I expected –"

"Expect? What's to expect? She's a skanky whore *and a junkie!*"

"I *know* she's a junkie! But, she needs my snitch money. She should be *early*. That's what I expect."

"So you think what little bit of cash you can toss her way will compete with what her line of work and that Jamaican boyfriend provides?" Klepp pointed to his crotch.

Jeez, thought Vale, *he's worse than I imagined. Multiple Internal Affairs investigations, a crippled partner from a botched collar, a couple tours through alcohol rehab, and he preaches as if he's the patron saint of cops. They said, "Humor him, gain his trust, find out how much he knows and where his loyalties lie." They didn't say he'd be such a prick. I swear he wants this case to go sideways just to piss me off. I'm sure glad he's having fun, because I certainly am not.*

Vale countered, "The trouble with you veterans is that you rely on the same old worn-out routines. You live on old-school prejudices, and –"

"What do you know, *College Boy*?"

"I *know* she's late, and –"

"Dammit! I *told* you why she's late. She's just another junkie."

"She's –" Vale attempted to continue.

"Whoa there, Rookie! Why are you so interested in this street twat? She's not Rasta Boy's number one girl. The one with the big tits is the one we should be leaning on. Or, maybe that little devil that does his recruiting. She's been flitting around in a lot of places across town, and –"

"– AS I WAS GOING TO SAY!" Vale blurted out.

Klepp shut up and stared at the younger cop. After a brief silence he laughed and said, "That took more balls than I thought you had. Good to see you begun to finally grow a pair."

Vale sighed, slumped and then continued, "Look, I *know* Francine is ready to cooperate."

"Really?"

"Yes, really. I know a lot about her."

"She your girlfriend, or something?"

"Get real."

Klepp gave him a sideways look and said, "Pussy is pussy."

"No way! Absolutely no way – I'm attached. And besides, I barely have time for anything but my job."

"Fine, College Boy, fine. You be Super Cop and save the world. Just tell me how you know that your Little Miss Skanky Pants is ready to cooperate?"

"She gets and spends her snitch money here every day at the same time.

"So?"

"Francine doesn't like playing number two to that big blonde, Glenda, who, by the way, is also a junkie. Glenda, the 'I wanna be a singer' that still has dreams of making it big. Glenda, Rasta Boy's number one."

"You know a lot about the female street scum around here. You sure you aren't bangin' some of it?"

Perry ignored the jab. "Francine told me all about Glenda."

"Really?"

"Yes, really! That's how I know she's planning some sort of move. I *know that because I do my job!*"

Klepp dripped sarcasm. "Makes me all warm inside knowing you are my new partner. Any more I should know?"

"You might want to know I tagged this next installment of snitch money. Whatever Francine makes, she eventually gives some to the Rasta Man. I can find and follow him and anyone else with the money." He held up a wad of bills and waved them at his partner.

"Rookie, I *am* impressed. How'd you tag the dough?"

"With RFID chips."

"Say what?"

"Microchips. High tech miniature bugs as small as a freckle."

Klepp was silent for a long time. Finally he asked, "Where does a rookie newbie like you get that kind of hi-tech new age backup?"

Oh shit, you idiot! Vale derided himself. *He'd be a moron not to suspect me after that slip-up. Think, man, think!*

"My kid brother!" he blurted. "He's a geek, you know, a techie. He's into all the latest stuff."

"Like how?"

"Well, like him and all the guys at his school, they –"

"Which school?"

"Ah...Rutgers. He goes to Rutgers."

Again, Klepp was silent for a while. After what seemed

ages, he said. "Good school. They finally started playing some real football. You a football fan, Rookie?"

"Me? Football? Yeah – yeah, I'm a fan, but I like the pros." *Good, he's sidetracked on sports.*

"Eagles? *Let me think. His brother? I thought he told me last week he was an only kid,* thought the veteran cop.

"Birds all the way! Is there any other team?" *Keep the old bastard talking!*

"Good, that's good, Rookie. Being loyal, being consistent, it's important. No matter who and what you are, it ain't nothing,' unless you show something in your character. It's what Francine ain't." *Ain't is right. As in this boy ain't right.*

"Ain't what?" Vale started to sweat through his shirt.

"It ain't consistent." *The kid is flustered. He's hiding something.*

"Consistent?" *Where's he taking this?*

"Yeah, consistent, loyal. You know, as in this instance, not being late." *I'll have to do some real sniffing into his background.*

"I get it." *I hope he doesn't keep at this.*

"No, that's what you rookies, with all your new high-tech crap, don't get." *I better lay back a bit. I don't want to tip him off that I think he smells funny.*

Klepp opened his newspaper and began scanning the sports page.

"What is it that we rookies do not get?" *He's faking interest in the paper.*

The veteran closed the sports section and said, "Look here, Rookie. Francine is just another low rent sleazy junkie. The only thing consistent about her is that she's going to screw up. Junkies like her, that's what they do. Face it, she ain't late. She ain't comin'." *Why is this newbie interested in her? She's a junkie whore doin' a phony flim-flam artist. And fuck him. How does this rookie rate technical backup of this caliber?*

"You make it sound so simple." *He's not giving up. He's suspicious.*

"It is simple." *I don't trust him. Better split him off on a wild goose chase and do some sniffing around on my own. Somebody placed him here with me – that I can smell like it's shit under my nose.*

"So, what do you suggest we do?" asked the rookie. *Maybe he'll tip me off to something.*

The senior cop reached across, opened the car door, and motioned for Vale to get out.

"You can try to find the broad while I rustle up a coffee and Danish." *I need to check in with people I know – find out about this punk – he definitely smells like a plant.*

"What?!" *He's dumping me?*

The young cop broke into a full sweat.

Klepp said, "If I can do anything to make things harder for you, Rookie, give me a call". *You piece-of-shit.*

"This is how you treat a partner?" the younger cop pleaded.

"Beat it, kid. I can't be wasting time on two-bit street trash like your girlfriend, Francine. I'll bet her lover-boy-the Rasta Man is out pimpin' that big-tit country hick he's always drivin' around with. You can wait – I'm outta here." *I gotta find out what side he's on.*

Rookie Detective Perry Vale got out as he was told. Before he could take a step his suspicious partner drove away.

Damn! The rookie detective thought. *He suspects me. I'm screwed.*

A HOLE TO THROW MONEY IN

Bud Delilah eyed the damaged vessel sitting in his boatyard. *Rogue waves can be a bitch – especially for these old-style wooden boats.* He moved his hand along the *Summerwind's* bowed mahogany planks feeling the damage it sustained from the freak occurrence. *But this one is solid – a real gem – well built and superbly maintained. McCoy really loved this boat, that's what saved her. That, and the Coast Guard.*

Across the parking lot a beat up truck pulled into a vacant spot. The truck's driver was immediately recognized by Bud.

That's Jersey Shore Joe alright. He's a bit grayer and a mite heavier than I remember him, but he seems ageless.

Joe got out of the beater and walked across the boatyard toward Bud. Upon arrival he gave Bud the "guy nod," and immediately got down to business. "Are you Bud?"

"That's me. I've been waiting for you, Joe." He extended his hand. "Good to know you are still kickin'."

"Barely, just barely." Joe looked beyond Bud at the damaged boat.

Bud responded to his interest. He pointed toward the thirty-six foot craft on blocks and hooked up to a misting system. "Are you seriously interested in a fix-me-up?"

"Yep. Tell me about her. How's she look?"

"Basically sound, but beat up," answered Bud. "She was close to going down. The Coasties did a good job getting her in."

Joe nodded his agreement and said, "It's kind of strange. When I saw the helo head out that night I think I

37

somehow knew I'd be connected to what was happening. I read about the incident and tracked the boat to here. All I can say is, 'God bless the Coast Guard.' I love wood boats, and I'm sure glad they saved this one." Joe focused his eye on the *Summer Wind*, and prodded Bud for details. "Give it to me, even the bad news. I fully understand that a boat can be a hole in the water where you toss your money."

"Water damage below was fairly serious. We pickled the engines quick. Saving them was the priority."

"Smart move. I'd have done the same," Joe said. "I'm a fair boatwright when I'm not spinning records. Tell me what needs to be done."

Bud eyed his clipboard. "We strip out the interior, all the water damaged material gets pulled, dry her out inside and refurbish below decks entirely. She needs new wiring and we have to sister three ribs. We fasten the loose planking and hope the pickling of the engines was done quick enough." He looked up at the misting system applying moisture to the hull and added, "Oh, yeah, as you can see, we keep her misted while in dry dock. Can't let her planks dry out."

"Sounds right," Joe said.

"Needs a bottom job, too," Bud added. "Caulking, sanding, finish work, and paint. Engines being pickled are still good. Oversized fuel tanks are new – no need to fool with 'em. That's all of it, I guess."

"Cost? What's the total?" asked Joe. "Purchase price included. You do the heavy work. I'll just supervise, help some, and hang out."

"Low end, fifty. High is seventy-five," Bob answered.

"Why the wide spread?"

Bob grinned. "High end is if you aren't the boatman you claim to be."

They both laughed.

Bud continued. "Workers with good wood skills are

getting scarce. If I have to bring someone else in it'll cost some more. If not, I can hit close to the lower number."

"How long?" asked Joe.

"Six weeks, maybe ten. It depends."

"Depends – on what?"

"Scheduled maintenance for my regulars. If they want something done, I've got to deliver."

"I understand. I'm a one-off customer. You've got to service your bread and butter accounts. I've got nothing but time. I can live with ten weeks."

"Good." said Bud. "Deal?"

Joe offered his hand. "Deal! When do we start?"

"You'll find me here as early as six. Have you found a place to stay nearby?"

Joe pulled a piece of paper from his pocket. "You know a B and B by the name of The Atlantic Inn? It's in Ocean City."

"Whoa! The Atlantic Inn," said Bud, "that's one of the nicest places around." He laughed and added, "Maybe I should have quoted a higher number for those repairs."

"Oh no, you got it wrong. I'm just working there, and it's just part-time. The decision to fix up this boat means I'm committing just about everything I have."

"If you love the old ones, that's the way it is."

"Yeah, don't I know that." Joe stood back and looked lovingly at the *Summer Wind*. "Just like music, the good old stuff takes all you've got."

BLINK, BLINK

Rasta Man Raff sat motionless on the edge of his bed. He was playing a macabre version of the child's game known as "Made You Blink." His opponent was winning. She was dead and would never blink again.

Raff thought as he stared, *"I can't stand it when they look at you like that. She's dead and still lookin' at me.*

He grabbed a soiled towel to toss over Francine's head and half-muttered, "Bitch, you got what you had coming."

Raff's crib was on the top floor of an almost dilapidated structure located on South Carolina Avenue a block from the beach. It was a few doors down from the sleazy motel where he conducted his business and housed his stable of women. At one time the three-story structure had been a stylish rooming house; now it served as Raff's personal sanctuary. Only a select few knew of its connection to him and his use of it as a retreat. "Down the street" is where he normally "did his thing." Usually the motel on the street would be teaming with the traffic of his drug-addicted young entourage, but earlier he had ordered them all to hit the pavement to find some fresh talent. Raff had told them he wanted to be alone with Francine.

The women did as they were told. They sensed that a shakeup was coming in their ranks and they hit the streets to recruit because bringing in a new member would stand one of them well with Raff. Francine had been quick to rise. One of them could move up just as she had.

On the streets they would size up the newcomers in town and do some talking – convincing a newbie to join them. Maybe one of them could show the skill needed to permanently replace the persuasive recruiter that had brought them in. If so, the lucky one could move up to front some parties and sell dope like Raff. Maybe even be like the recruiter and leapfrog over Raff himself to deal with the higher-ups. Rumor had it that she made it far enough to be in on the big transaction that was about to come down.

Hadn't Francine hinted about it? But word was that she was in serious trouble for something. When Raff singled Francine out and split with her "down the street" he had ordered the rest of them to hit the streets. Something was up, but they had no knowledge of the deadly child's game that had just concluded.

~ ~ ~

Raff wiped his bloodied fingertips on the towel and emitted a sick laugh, just like the ones he made while burying the girl under the boardwalk.

Francine was busy working on me. She was thinkin' I was into her as my new top bitch and never saw me grab for it Wham! An ice pick in the ear will teach her to play me.

Raff saw a bead of blood on her ear lobe and shouted at the dead girl, "I told you never to cross me!" He fingered the towel nervously and dabbed the blood away.

Francine answered him with her continued silent stare. Raff, with Just Tony and Joey still on his mind and the girl before him, shook to his core.

Those greasers are a joke to everybody but themselves. That's why they are so dangerous – they believe their own shit.

He shouted at her again. "Them white boys – *they* made me do it, girl! *They* the ones!"

He covered Francine's eyes and face with the bloodstained towel and winced. Raff's scarred fingertips were still raw from the digging under the boardwalk.

Mother Fuck! All I need now is another digging session under that bunch of rotten boards. I'll bury you later. I got more important things to do, like keeping myself alive and out'a reach of them white boys thinkin' they are some bad-ass mafia like on TV.

Raff began yet another one of his gruesome tasks. He folded Francine's arms across her chest, grabbed her ankles, and pulled her to the staircase. Then he dragged her down two flights of stairs. At the basement doorway he shoved the still warm body down the final short flight of stairs into the dark.

If she told those two grease balls about me.... What if she talked to somebody else? I got to find who she's been talkin' to... Like, maybe that cop always hangin' around the neighborhood. But first, I got to find some new girls to get those thugs off my ass. That bitch who brung me them preppy little pussies is long gone. I gotta hustle or get my bitches to find new meat. Gotta get a young one for Fat Ass Joey. Everything will be good then. All them greaseballs care about is sellin' pussy and dope to horny white tourists. That and being racist pigs.

Raff cautiously climbed down the darkened stairs, stepped over Francine, and began rummaging in the basement. When he located a plastic mattress cover and a length of rope he returned to the tumbled body and spoke to it as he worked.

"You're going in the freezer. I'll bury you in the sand, later."

Raff hog-tied the lifeless form in a tight fetal position, pushed it into the oversized plastic bag, and wrapped it into as small a bundle as possible. Finally, he dumped her into the freezer as if she were Saturday's special at the market.

"Enough room in there for you?" Raff asked as he stuffed the body toward the bottom and kept talking. "Damn it, bitch, you finally did slim down." He emitted another of his sick snickers. "'Nuff room in there for you *and* a friend. Stay there and chill out."

Laughing fully, he slammed the freezer shut and scurried up the stairs. At the doorway, he secured the basement entrance with a chain and padlock and murmured, "Nobody gonna be peekin' in and findin' you!"

From behind a familiar voice asked, "*Nobody* is going to find *who*?"

Raff whirled just in time to see the cop's fist crash into his face. Before he could fall, a knee was crammed into his still tender groin. He went limp.

"Maybe I should check out what's in your basement," the cop said.

A second blow hit Raff's face and he dropped to the floor.

"That's a reminder from your bosses to find the girls you owe them."

HEARTH AND HOME

The newly retired DJ eyed the scrap of paper in his hand to reconfirm the address. Satisfied that he had it right, he eased his battered old truck into the parking spot directly in front of the Atlantic Inn.

"This is it," Joe said to himself. Joe inspected the inn and wondered how a burnout like him would fit in such an upscale establishment. He got out for a better look.

Sitting two blocks from the beach on a large corner lot across from a modern high school and a park, the Atlantic Inn was a century-old structure that had recently undergone a total renovation. In the past it had been a mansion, a way station for Philadelphia's beach going day-trippers, and then a flophouse. Now it was a luxury bed and breakfast hotel with all the trimmings.

At the top of the stairs an attractive thirty-something woman waved and asked, "What do you think of it, Uncle Joe?

"It has character alright." He replied. "You've done well, Marie. I'm amazed. What a place you've got here!"

"I'm glad you like your new home."

Joe froze when the words hit him.

Marie shouted, "*Surprised?*"

Joe remained frozen.

Marie giggled and asked, "Has the cat got your tongue, Uncle Joe?"

Joe still did not move. Finally, he said, "Did I hear you right? I'm staying here? I mean I'm working *and living here*?"

"Of course," Marie answered. She came down the stairs and gave him a hug.

He remained stiff. She hugged him again. He melted.

"I just thought you were giving me a place to work part-time while I sort out my options. I was thinking of fixing up a boat – then retiring altogether. Are you sure it's okay for me to stay? I can find a place on my own."

"That's silly, Uncle Joe. I can't have my most famous relative living anywhere else in Ocean City. I only agreed to the handyman gig to lure you to our wonderful community. I had to get you here somehow." She hugged her uncle a third time and he melted even more.

Grinning shyly Joe said, "I've only stayed away because this place is dry."

"I know. No beach bars means no Jersey Shore Joe." She laughed and hugged him yet again. "You'll love it here, and Ocean City will love you right back!"

"I hope so."

"You know – we do have radios. And more than a few people have heard of you here in Ocean City."

"*Really?*"

"It may shock you, but Jersey Shore Joe's radio shows have been as popular here as anywhere else along the shore."

"Even that last stinker on the graveyard shift?"

"Even that one."

"That's hard for me to imagine. I didn't think that one had more than a handful of listeners. The Arbitron numbers on it were the worst I ever posted. Just terrible – and they would have driven me off the air if I hadn't quit. I'm done."

"Done or not – from now on Ocean City is your home."

"I...I don't, I...don't ..." Joe turned away to hide a moist eye. "I really don't know what to say."

Marie spun him around, hugged him as hard as she could, and said, "Just say, 'I'll catch you later down on the Boardwalk.'"

GETTING BY

Lil DeNova was anxious and upset. She was always queasy after Joey Valentine came for one of his visits. Her unease was well founded. As she thought about her situation she fidgeted with the items on her desk.

I make a good living selling top quality merchandise to the high-end tourist market, but the real money comes from what Joey brings me. I don't know where he gets these items and I really don't care. But I know the merchandise is tainted and I just can't have anyone learn about where it comes from.

Lil tried to convince herself that all was well.

Ocean City is a family resort community – who would ever connect my shop with Joey and his fast-paced doings in Atlantic City? AC is a world apart from what goes on here.

Through the open office door she gazed at her store's merchandise.

Nobody is getting hurt – it's just me selling estate jewelry and expensive rags. It's just business, that's what it is, business. Besides, I have to survive.

Her bread-and-butter, *Lil's Consignment Boutique,* was located on Asbury Avenue in the center of a small group of upscale establishments. Lil's specialty was catering to the wealthier visitors that shopped in the district. She had been the owner fifteen years – ever since her husband, Vincent Valentine, was killed in a robbery attempt. He was the robber, an inept robber. The intended victim fought back.

Lil sighed and fingered the jewelry left by Joey.

I've been successful in putting the past behind me, she thought. *No one here asks about my years of marriage to Vincent, his end, or my time scamming gamblers in AC. Thank God. So, why do I keep the relationship alive?* She looked at the picture of herself, Vincent, and their son that she kept near the register. *It's simple*, she told herself. *Family ties trump everything else. I go along with Joey, fence his stuff, and close one eye because it's family business.* She marched through the store.

The spot Lil selected for the jeweled mermaids was in a storefront showcase. Lil draped the pendant around a neck-stand by its chain and laid the earrings on a matching piece of black felt directly below.

There, she observed with a smile, *I'll get twenty-five hundred for these beauties in no time. I'll tell Joey my usual weepy tale of how cheap the tourists are, and explain that two thousand was all I could squeeze out of some guy trying to impress his wife. Joey will split the sale, seventy-thirty, taking the lion's share for himself. With the hidden extra, my take on these little swimmers should be eleven hundred. Not bad. What could be wrong with that? I may be living in a wholesome tourist town, but I haven't forgotten my street-savvy ways learned in AC.*

She returned to the office and sat at her desk. Lil's eyes landed on the local newspaper lying before her. She frowned. The *Ocean City Gazette* confronted her with the reality of her life's dilemma.

Good people, families, this place is full of them. Folks are so proud to be from here that they travel with copies of the Gazette to have their pictures taken with it in front of landmarks and tourist sites around the world. Guilt rushed out her every pore. *I'm such a phony. No one suspects that I was such a tramp and a thief.* The image of two happy middle-aged couples at the Louvre stared at her. *I'm not them – but I am not what I was either. I'm not a...a...a... No – no! That's not me anymore. That life is behind me.*

Lil picked up the newspaper and quickly stuffed it in the trash.

HOME SWEET HOME

The more Joe learned about the Atlantic Inn the more he liked it. *This place could grow on a guy,* he told himself. *The reconstruction work is first rate, so my job as a handyman is a breeze. It's in a superb location and the guests are wonderful.*

Joe looked out on Ocean City from the hotel's rooftop deck. His gaze stopped two blocks to the east where a Jersey Shore landmark presided over the boardwalk.

That Ferris wheel serves as a great beacon. I can understand how it saved the boat. Too bad time ran out for McCoy. I wonder what he was doing alone, at sea, at night, in the off-season's rough seas.

Joe scanned the city he now called home.

Ocean City is as perfect a place as I could find. Imagine, all those years on the Shore and I stayed away because I thought my music was good only when it was lubricated with alcohol. In my youth, how much was I like those louts on that idiotic TV program?

A familiar Shore song by the Smithereens, *House We Used to Live In*, provided the soundtrack for his thoughts. Engrossed in his musing, Joe did not hear his niece's arrival.

Marie tapped his shoulder. "It's not like you to let me, or anyone else, sneak up on you, Uncle Joe."

"Maybe I'm getting hard of hearing in my dotage," he joked.

"Some dotage...rebuilding a boat...writing your memoirs –"

Surprised by her knowledge of his doings, Joe asked, "How'd you know I was dabbling in writing about my sordid past?"

"Ocean City may have more than a hundred and fifty thousand residents during the summer, but during this time of year we three thousand full-time islanders are a tight-knit group. Two members of your writing group are friends of mine. They get their hair done at the same place I do."

"Amazing. So, if I find a girlfriend will you know about that too?"

"Yes, and probably before you."

"Good God, I don't believe it." He grinned. "Wait. I do believe it. This place is unreal."

"I told you it *can* grow on you."

"It already has. I think I'm beginning to sincerely appreciate Ocean City."

"I told you so."

"You also told me, 'it's the place where people who want to get away go to get away from the people who want to get away.'"

"That's true, but even more so in the off season."

"Which can be slow. At your age I would have balked at being here. Hell – I did."

"I don't mind the pace."

"And, that prompts me to ask – why did you 'go all in' and buy this place, the inn? You had such a great business career ahead of you. Weren't you in line to manage a big hotel in New York?"

"I've known about this place for years – ever since I worked here as a kid."

"You worked here?"

"My first job fresh out of high school was making beds in the *old* Atlantic Inn. It was quite a sight back then. The Paxtons bought it from the people who ran it when I first worked here. Then they did the massive rehab and turned it into a Bed and Breakfast. By chance I met them at a hotel management conference a couple of years ago. In our conversations I mentioned how I started my hotel career in Ocean City – at the very place they owned. For some reason we kept in touch after the meeting and when I learned they were considering a well-deserved world tour as a reward for all their hard work, I pitched the idea of them selling it to me. I was surprised they said 'yes' after all the effort they put into this place. Me owning this place was meant to be. You know, it has to be synchronicity."

"Like me leaving that last gig and ending up here?"

"It couldn't have been planned better by God himself – unless you had been washed ashore. So here you are – Jersey Shore Joe on the best part of the Jersey Shore." She waved toward the ocean. "Beautiful, right?"

"Scary is more like it," said Joe.

"Scary?"

"The Jersey Shore is a hundred and forty miles long, and all along its length – every so many of those miles – somebody claims that that particular location is the best spot on the shore."

"What's so scary about that?"

"They're all right."

"All of them? But, that can't be."

"I know – that's why it's scary. Anyone who goes 'down the shore' is a fierce loyalist for their own particular stretch of sand. You can imagine how that always put me in a tough spot."

"Why?"

"Just imagine being *Jersey Shore* Joe."

"I see. Everyone laid claims to you – just like their own stretch of sand."

"Yes...and I let them...without ever picking my own spot."

"So pick one now – pick Ocean City."

"Maybe. I'll let you know when I'm ready."

LITTLE GIRL LOST

The girl, a runaway from *The Sisters of Sorrows School* in Mays Landing, stood across the street from the trendy boutique and fumed. She knew for certain that the woman in the shop was not telling the truth.

Damn it! She's lying – I know it, the girl told herself. *That woman couldn't be mistaken about the jewelry's background because she's flat out lying – and I know it!*

The angry young woman crossed Asbury Avenue and headed in the general direction of the Atlantic Inn. In her mind she replayed her visit and what she saw.

She kept on telling me the same story that the jewelry was from a local islander's estate. I know better. That mermaid pendant and earrings are unique. One-of-a-kind originals is what they are; made in Florida years ago for a special once-in-lifetime occasion. I ought to know.

She balled up her fists and tensed her body. *Damn it! I want them!*

As the girl walked, the she re-played other events in her head.

After their New Year's "Escape to New York" went awry, two ex-school girls, Jessie Collier and Brooke Paxton, had found themselves stranded in a seedy club on Ocean Boulevard in Long Branch, on the upper portion of the Jersey Shore.

We'd never been that far up the shore before, she recalled. *We both wanted to hit the bars and stops made famous in the old days – like The Stone Pony – and the new ones you see on TV. Good looks, no money, and no plan – what a combination.*

She smiled.

Those guys we hitched a ride were pissed when they figured out we were 'not putting out.' They expected a lot from us just for their agreeing to drive us up the shore and on to Times Square in Manhattan.

She smiled more as she remembered her friend.

Those guys were shocked at how tough we were. We kicked one of 'em in the nuts for trying to put the moves on us, and then arm choked his pal as he came to the rescue.

She repeatedly chanted. *That's how it happened – that's how it happened.*

She paused to think. *I've got to remember it just like that – as it happened – that's it.*

She smiled, but it quickly faded as she thought more about her friend. *It wasn't like her to get that interested in a third-rate musician. I was surprised that she was talking to a reggae dude with the entourage of trashy looking girls. But he impressed her with talk of her singing with his group. It was too noisy in the club for me to hear all his spiel. It must have been good. She obviously fell for it. We never saw New York. Parties and hustling. Parties and hustling.*

The girl frowned and her thoughts took her back to how they landed in Atlantic City. *When the local cops came in to check IDs, we hid in the ladies room. The owner of the club was about to give us up. That was just before the cops swept through again, they would have nabbed both of us if it weren't for the Rasta Man hustling us away. Damn him!*

Her frown increased.

I did some low shit in Atlantic City. But I got out, she didn't. Never, never, never again. God, we were tight. Everyone saw it – they had to – the way she and I were almost identical. "Sisters from other mothers" we called it. Everyone confused us for each other.

She stared at the shop.

That jewelry was what bound us together, and I will get it!

She took stock of her situation and resources.

I've only got a few dollars, a change of clothes, and the spare key to the Atlantic Inn's storeroom. The new owners aren't due to show up for a couple more weeks. If the key still works, I'll camp out there and figure something out. Passing by that shop's display window was fate. I was led there. She again looked back in the direction of the shop. *I'm going to get that jewelry – I'm going to get that jewelry.*

The task she faced did not scare her.

I've dealt with worse.

Emboldened by the challenge she told herself, *I'll never have to go back to what I was. I'll never give up. I'm not going to fail – I'm not going to fail!*

BEHIND THE EIGHT BALL

Joey Valentine positioned the better part of his oversized waistline on the pool table's rail and leaned in for a final shot. "Eight ball in the corner. For another C note – right?" He aimed a gloating smile at his friend.

"Just shut up and shoot, fat-ass," Just Tony snapped. "How come every fuckin' time it's for a C note? And then you run the fuckin' table!"

"It's clean livin', 'Tony – clean livin'." He flashed another smile. "Clean living...and I go to confession once a week."

He took the shot, made it, and did a little dance.

Carapelli tossed a folded bill onto the table. "That's three fuckin' games in a row."

Joey stopped dancing, snatched the bill, and held it close to his face. He spoke to it as a friend. "Like I told him, Mr. Franklin, I'm livin' right, and – "

His phone vibrated.

To the face on the C note Joey said, "Excuse me, Ben. I gotta take this call." He looked at the phone, and recognizing the number, explained to Just Tony, "It's one of our cop pals."

"Which one?"

"The kid."

"Good. You think he did that little cleanup?" Tony questioned.

"We'll soon find out how clean things are." Joey flipped the phone open and put its speaker on. "Talk to *us*," he said to the caller.

"Are you both there? Am I on the speaker?"

"Yeah," Just Tony said loud enough to reach the phone in Joey's hand. "You got a problem with that?"

"No – yes – no – I mean –"

Just Tony repeated, "*You* got a problem with *that*?"

There was silence on the phone.

"Good!" Just Tony barked at the silence. "Now, tell us something we want to hear."

"Okay – Okay." The caller sighed and said, "I checked on the girl. She's dead."

"You certain?" asked Joey.

"Yes, yes. I saw her. He stashed the body in a freezer – plans to take care of it later."

"He better. You see to it!"

"I will. I will. I'll see to it."

"You better," Joey said again for emphasis.

"Think he's clear on what he's supposed to do?" Just Tony asked.

With bravado the caller asserted, "Damn right! I delivered our message again – real hard – knocked the bastard out. When he came to – like I told you – he showed me the girl."

"You better be right," Just Tony said with menace.

"I'm one hundred percent certain. I peeled back the plastic she's in and checked up close. It was her – she's not a problem – not anymore." The caller's voice cracked.

"Meaning what?" Just Tony asked.

"Well – ah – I – ah –"

"Spit it out," said Just Tony.

"It's my new partner – I'm worried. Something isn't right. I think he's been paired with me for surveillance."

"So, take care of it," Joey cut in.

"Take care of it? How?"

"Get rid of him." Just Tony ordered.

"What?"

"You deaf?"

"Wait – wait. I'm not ..."

"You're not *what*?" Just Tony pressed.

"I'm – I'm – not a m – m – murderer. I'm –"

"You are whatever we say you are!" Just Tony told him. "And, you'll do whatever we tell you. Just as soon as that phony Jamaican beefs up our stable of girls, find a new manager – a less visible type. Rasta Boy is a good recruiter, but he's become a liability. You stick to him like glue. Make sure he's doing just what we told him. When he's done filling the order – get rid of him, *and* your new partner. Both of them, the cop and that dope-pushing pimp. The two of them need to go away. Do it! Make it look like a bust gone bad."

"Yeah," Joey chimed in, "if you have to – sacrifice some of the product. Make it look real. Just don't use up too much stuff – we got a business to run."

"But – but –"

"But, *what*!?" yelled Just Tony. "Don't act like some innocent kid. You and us – we have a relationship that goes back a long way. Don't kid yourself – you always knew something like this it would come up. You are on the inside for a reason. So, do your cop thing."

"But – but – b ..."

The call ended when Just Tony waved for his companion. After the big man flip-closed his phone, he asked, "You think he's got the balls to do both the pimp *and* the cop?"

"He better. That's all I can say – he better."

"You want me to cover him with somebody else – for insurance?"

"Yeah – but set it up in person. Meet with the other one yourself. Two cops going after one cop ought to work."

Lover Boy Joey smiled, and said, "Sure, Tony, sure. No problem."

OLD FRIENDS

Big Boy Johnny Klepp winked, eased his large frame past the secretary in the outer office, and without knocking strutted through the doorway into the office of the Director of Police Personnel. Inside, he flashed a smile at the surprised occupant behind the large desk.

"Clammy, my love," he purred, "I've got a little favor to ask."

Captain Mary Clamson shot her ex-partner an icy stare. "You've got a lot of nerve showing up here unannounced, Klepp."

The intruder kicked the door shut, positioned himself on the edge of the desk, and leaned forward pushing his face inches away from Mary.

"Shut...your...yap," he growled and grinned ending in a leering stare.

Mary countered with a colder version of her original stare. Klepp did not move and stared back with at least equal intensity. After a considerable time, Klepp spoke without breaking his stare. "Looks like a stand-off."

Mary Clamson was unaffected. "Only if you flinch, asshole."

Klepp's stare drifted downward. "I like your tits." He hissed the last word and remained focused on her cleavage like snake preparing to strike.

"You are one depraved letch," she hissed back.

"Yeah," Klepp sighed, "I guess I am." He kept his focus on her chest and inched closer. He flicked his tongue repeatedly, then said, "So, how 'bout a taste, Clammy?"

She answered with a sharp right-handed smack. "Not if you keep calling me that damned name!"

Mary attempted a second blow with her other hand,

but her left hook was severely limited in range and he caught it easily before it landed on his cheek. "Damn!" she cried, as Klepp fended off the blow. "I can't even get the pleasure of hitting you with a one-two like in the old days."

"Teach you right for taking a bullet in that arm. You should have ducked."

"If I had ducked you'd be planted in City Cemetery instead of smelling up my office." She leaned forward and landed a quick and decidedly friendly kiss on his lower lip. "I have to admit – all in all – I do miss you," she told him.

Klepp licked his lips, "Mmmmm...not bad. Maybe a bit wet – or clammy, *Clammy.*"

This time she connected solidly with her right. The smack was loud and her hand created a visible red mark on his cheek. "You know how I hate being called that name! I told you when we were partners – don't call me that!"

Klepp rubbed his face as he moved to her side of the desk.

"Sorry, *Mary,* my love. I was just having a little fun."

"Fun? Your sense of fun sucks."

"There ya go getting me a riled up talkin' about sucking."

"Stop it, damn you! Just stop it!"

He gave her a phony hurt look. "Maybe I should just step outside and come in again. You know – drag in here, all sad-assed and pussy-whipped, like all those weak spineless dopes on the force wanting to slip it to you. Maybe then – if you want – you'll trade a favor for some dick." He rubbed his groin and writhed, making a deranged face.

"Stop it!"

Keeping the face, he said, "I hear B...B...Billy C...C...Coyle h...h...has a t...t...thing f...f...for you."

"Johnny – Pa – leez!"

"Okay, okay. I hear you."

Mary tried to veer the conversation by picking up on the person in his comment. "Look, I'm way too old for Bill Coyle. Everyone knows he's only interested in the young stuff. The world will be ending when you see me with him. Besides, he's not my type either."

"God, I love it when you see it my way." With one big arm he drew her near.

"Johnny, stop. I'm not interested – not any more. That kiss was just for 'Hello.'" She reached behind. "Now, get your hand off my ass! What if someone came in and saw us?" She broke his hold and he stepped back.

"Sure, sure. Have it your way," he said. "But if someone caught me feeling your butt, they'd assume we were back to our old ways – humpin' like rabbits in spring."

She shushed him by placing her hand over his mouth. "Hold it down – *please!*"

"Yes'm," he mumbled as he eased into a chair. "I'll be good – I promise."

She changed the subject. "You mentioned a favor – are you short on cash again?"

"No...no...nothing like that." He pointed to her computer.

"No way!" she barked. "The last time you used my password it caused a mega stink. The IT manager called Internal Affairs and the new guy they have up there has been looking sideways at me ever since."

"That only happened because you were out of town. Some nerdy programmer matched your vacation time with the log-in and...well, you know....they naturally saw it as a slight breech in security."

"Slight? You make it sound – so – so –"

"Natural?" He flashed another grin. "This time I got it covered. Trust me."

"Yeah, genius, explain it to me."

"It's simple. You login now...take a potty break...and I stay. That way, there's no discrepancy with your schedule."

She had that look a person gets when they agree even if they don't want to. "Well..."

"I promise, this is the last time I ask for a favor, ever. All I need is a couple minutes."

"For what?"

"It's better if you not know."

"Shit!"

"I'll take that for a 'yes.'" Klepp smiled like a cheating winner.

Mary picked up her purse and headed toward the door. On the way, she dodged his attempt to land another kiss, but failed to avoid a pat on the rear as she grabbed the doorknob. "I'm already logged-in," she told him. "I'll be back in fifteen minutes – don't be here when I return."

He was at the computer before the door closed.

"My, my, my," Klepp murmured, as he scanned Mary's e-mails, "the girl has moved on indeed. She's no longer interested in me for good cause – she's boinkin' an assistant DA *and* a casino big wig. Mary's been sporting a lot of expensive jewelry lately. She always liked the baubles. I'll bet Clammy has some other sucker on the line – one with plenty of dough." He chided himself for getting off track. "Better hurry – she'll be back soon."

Klepp opened the secured personnel folders and immediately went to the V's. When he landed on Perry Vale's information he was not surprised by what he found. *My gut was right,* he told himself. *I know he's been lying through his teeth. That rookie is a plant! The question is who put him here, and why?*

The veteran detective lovingly patted the computer above its screen. *There it is – the item that points out the lie. How can an only child have a geek brother at*

Rutgers? I saw how he was sweating when he told me that line of crap. He smiled then quickly frowned. *Why the fuck did he land in my lap? That's all what I want to know.*

Klepp knew exactly where to look and quickly scrolled through the confidential addendums sent by the State Police. *I've got to hand it to him – the sneaky little prick has some interesting and powerful friends, and the pedigree to be the perfect rat. His friends certainly own him.*

Klepp looked at his watch. *Time to go. Better scatter some leaves on my trail.*

He quickly scanned some additional files and slapped a sticky note on the computer screen. As agreed, he was gone before Mary returned.

In less than five minutes Captain Mary Clamson was back at her desk retracing the steps Klepp had taken in his research. She too found what she was looking for. She grabbed the phone and made a call.

"Listen to this," she said. "John Klepp paid me a visit."

"For?"

"He wanted to nose through my computer again – so I let him."

"What got his interest?"

"He looked at the records of all his ex-partners, including me."

"Cut to the end."

"I think he drew a blank. He stopped his search on the detailed retirement info only HR is supposed to see. I got a note from him saying "thanks," and hinting that he's going to write a memoir of his career as a cop. Imagine that – the fool can barely sign his name and he's thinks he can be an author."

"So...what's the harm?"

"None. I don't think we should worry about him – he

doesn't suspect a thing. He's in the dark and doesn't know it."

"See to it that he stays there."

Before Mary could reply the person she called hung up.

GOTCHA!

Raff looked out the side window of the van and whispered, "Keep joggin', baby, don't pay me no mind. Keep joggin,' baby – just keep joggin'."

Under pressure and in a desperate effort to fulfill Joey Valentine's order for a young girl, Raff had moved his "recruiting activities" north along the Shore to upscale Long Beach Island. After several failures to lure young girls into his van he decided stronger and more direct measures had to be taken. He would snatch a girl off the street.

"Let that fat pig, Joey, and his fowl mouthed partner deal with the fallout," he thought as he watched the girl.

Raff's mind raced as they passed the unaware target. Second thoughts pelted him.

This is beyond risky! It's crazy! I always had others doin' shit like this. Too much pressure – that fat-assed white boy wants a baby bitch that's fresh – wants it fast. Shit! There ain't no un-popped slits to be found in all of AC. I can recruit all the pussy we need for the casinos, but finding a cherry in New Jersey who is over sixteen is damned near impossible.

Raff continued to eye his prey.

I hope that pig-faced greaser is happy with this one. It looks like she's fourteen maybe fifteen. All I can say is, she better be untouched. But there's no way to tell while she's on the shelf. I've got to get the merchandise home to know for sure. He better like 'em doped up, because that's the only way I can nab and deliver this one.

He decided to make his move.

Damn, I hate kidnapping. I gave up strong-arm stuff when I left Chicago. Dealing dope and burying other people's mistakes is my thing.

He continued to watch the girl.

But, it's you or me – it's you or me.

He barked instructions to Glenda, his lead girl, companion, and driver.

"Go past her. Do the speed limit – no more!" He pointed ahead. "See that driveway up there – the one with the fancy-assed painted fish on the mailbox?"

Glenda nodded and aimed the van where she was told.

"Pull in there and come back out and then go back toward her," he ordered. "Don't look at her – keep your eyes straight ahead."

Glenda complied, and soon the van rolled past the young girl listening to an IPod while she exercised. "I take it we'll come back for the grab?" she clarified.

"Yeah – yeah. Just do as I say. Easy does it, and don't go fast."

They moved just under the speed limit north on Long Beach Boulevard passing from the beach community of Harvey Cedars into, Loveladies, the next small borough. It was an off-season morning and little traffic was on LBI's beach road. The island community was the last place anyone would attempt what Raff was about to do. That's exactly why he was there.

It would have been better to nab her up the road near the convent. But, Glenda is Catholic, and she bitched up a storm. Fuck, we're nabbin' a kid off the street and she gets all religious on me!

At the colorful mailbox Glenda pulled in, turned the van about, exited the driveway, and headed south toward the girl. The jogging girl was headed away from the van and had not seen the vehicle turn around. In seconds they were upon her.

Raff remained cool. "You know what to do," he said, "*so do it.*"

Raff grabbed a handkerchief and doused it with chloroform as Glenda steered the van into position and quickly stopped next to the girl. He whipped open the sliding door and jumped out.

Instead of fleeing, the girl froze. It was a terrible mistake.

Before she could emit a scream Raff had the girl's mouth covered and she wilted as he shuffled her into the van. It was all over in seconds.

THE MOUSE

Joe savored the salt-seasoned air by inhaling it deeply, holding his breath, and slowly expelling it through his nose. After several repetitions he stopped to eye his surroundings. Joe was seated on one of the memorial benches positioned along the Ocean City boardwalk watching the morning parade of bikers, walkers and joggers.

The crowd is thick for so early in the day, even for a weekend. And it's still winter. I can't imagine the crowds this place draws during the summer. I'd like it to stay this way forever. I know the ten or eleven weeks from July 4th through Labor Day are crucial for business, but I like this boardwalk when it's quiet because the population is sparse.

His left arm was draped along the message engraved on the bench's top rail. It read: "Lolly, our little angle watching over us."

The two and a half mile length of Ocean City's boardwalk was peppered with similar benches; each with its own personal message. Joe liked sitting in the mornings at the "Lolly Bench," as he called it. His favorite afternoon perch was further north, beyond the lone high-rise building, at the intersection of "the boards" and DeLancey Street. There, "Stella and Moon" were forever remembered. Joe had no idea who they were. He liked not knowing.

While seated on his favorite benches Joe liked to make up stories to fit the names. In his tales Lolly, Stella, and Moon were simple and quiet folk who loved the boardwalk. Without trying, and even without his noticing Joe was being absorbed by Ocean City in a level deeper

71

than he could ever have experience through music. The community's beach house-lined streets had combined with sun, sand, and salt spray to marinate his being and transform his essence. He felt that he was truly becoming a new person.

This place is so different from Atlantic City. That boardwalk is all hustle and bustle. It is street performers, panhandlers, foot taxis, and tourists. AC's boardwalk has a big-city feel, like an office worker on a shadowy lark – sneaking out to gamble, toss down a drink, and maybe get a quickie. On the periphery there is a crowd of street-wise parasites ready to snatch the crumbs that literally and figuratively fall off the casinos gaming tables. Compared to the laid-back family-oriented no-booze bubble protecting Ocean City, AC is Sodom and Gomorrah.

He looked north the dozen miles "as the crow flies" to study the Atlantic City skyline.

From here the hotels and casinos look like a gray and beige mountain range reaching into the sea. It's too far away to see the wooden apron of the boardwalk. The two boardwalks are as different as can be. Here, parents can let their kids roam free, but AC's boards are not as safe. Then again, it's not the same people. Up in AC the casinos actually have to broadcast how-to-videos advising patrons not to abandon their children while gambling. I guess that is to be expected when the city's folklore includes a four hour eighteen minute stretch when some guy rolled consecutively 154 times at the dice table.

Joe looked about where his new life was being formed.

I love it here. I really do. Give me the Doo Dah Parade with its 500 Basset hounds any day of the week over the casino's parade of losers...and I don't even like dogs.

He smiled as he remembered watching the Beach Chair Drill Team and the entries in the Basset Hound

Waddle during the last Doo Dah. To anyone passing by, Joe appeared as a man totally at peace.

Today, I'll work a while on the boat, write some about my memories, and forget for another day that I had a life before coming here. Maybe I'll go another day without being called Jersey Shore Joe. I am happy to just be plain Joe.

Joe absent-mindedly massaged his leg and spent the next minutes observing the people traveling to and fro. A colorful jumble of shoes, hats, and sweatpants bobbed, swayed and wiggled past him on the well-marked lanes of the popular beachfront path. After a few minutes of therapy, Joe rose and began negotiating the bike and foot traffic. Although his legs ached more often than not, Joe seldom missed his daily five-mile to and fro tour of the boardwalk.

When Joe reached the Ferris wheel he turned inland and stayed on the south side of the street opposite the skate board arena. Just inside the arena fence several young boys with too much testosterone were showing off for no one in particular. As Joe passed the arena his eye caught a waving signal coming from Marie down the street. He broke into his best "old man's jog" and covered the distance to the inn more quickly than he could have only a few weeks before.

"You're just the man I want to see," greeted Marie. She pointed toward the door to the inn's storeroom. "I believe I've cornered a mouse."

"A mouse?" He gave her a blank look.

"I need some help. It's a big one."

"Marie, I've seen you in action. You certainly don't need my help with a mouse."

She held her hand as high as his head. "I said a big one. I think I might have a people-type mouse. Maybe it's one of the kids from the high school."

"Whoa – even if it is – I'm not qualified."

"You'll do fine." She gave him the "pretty please" smile and pointed again at the storeroom.

"Okay," Joe said with a very cautious tone. "But, fill me in on what you think you have here. I need to know what I'm getting into."

"I noticed some things were moved about as if someone was sleeping in there. I think whoever it is scurried into the shadows to hide when I entered."

"That's easy enough to find out," Joe said with a shrug. He walked to the door, pounded, yanked it open, and leaned inside. In a booming voice he shouted, "Attention! This is Officer Stevens of the Ocean City Police! I am a K-9 officer and have my dog with me! I'm releasing him in thirty seconds! I advise you to vacate the property immediately!"

There was shuffling in the shadows. A voice cried out, "Okay! Okay! I'm...I'm...com...com...coming out! Just give me a minute!"

Joe pounded the door and woofed like a hungry hound. Out of the dark, a terrified girl burst through the doorway. She halted as soon as she realized only Marie and Joe were present.

"Damn!" exclaimed the girl. "You lied. Where's the dog?"

Joe looked at Marie, grinned, and said, "My job's done – there's your mouse."

The girl looked confused. "Mouse?" she asked, looking back into the storeroom. "You mean mice are in there?"

"No – kid," said Joe. "You're the mouse...and I'm *not* a cop." He nodded to Marie and said, "I'll let you sort this out. She looks pretty tame to me. I'll be at the boat yard if you need me." Joe waved, and quickly left.

Marie waited until Joe was out of range. Focusing on the girl, she made an appraisal.

She looks harmless enough. A bit ragged – figures if she's been living here in there. Seventeen – I say, or there about.

Sternly Marie said, "I'll give you thirty seconds to tell me why you've been hiding in my storeroom. If it's not one hell of a tale – you get to repeat it to the real cops."

The girl, a slim brunette with close-cropped hair, drew in a breath, closed her eyes, and said, "My name is Brooke – Brooke Paxton. I –"

"Hold it!" Marie interrupted. "Paxton? As in Earl and Lynne Paxton?"

The girl gulped and said, "Yeah – yeah. I guess you could say so."

Marie's demeanor softened. "From what I know, your parents probably think you are safe at school. You are supposed to be there, right?"

"Well...ah, yes."

The girl started to cry. Marie's sternness faded immediately. She reached out and with a hug said "Okay, Brooke. It's okay. Just take some deep breaths and relax."

The girl did as instructed. In moments she recovered.

"Thanks," The girl said softly. "Thanks... ah...ah ..."

"Marie – I'm Marie. I'm the Inn's new owner. Your folks sold it to me. That's how I know about where you should be." She paused, and then asked, "Brooke, do you think you are calm enough to tell me what brought you here?"

Sheepishly Brooke replied, "Okay – sure." She took a breath, closed her eyes and began telling her tale of running away from The Sisters of Sorrows School. Marie listened with interest.

"I – ah – ah – I mean, Jessie – even though she graduated a couple of years ago – we're best friends anyway. We hung out together because, well even though she is older than me, we look so much alike. A lot of times, people couldn't tell us a part because – . Wait!" She cried out, "Wait, I can show you."

She disappeared into the storeroom, shouting over her shoulder, "I'll get my things and show you!" In a few moments she re-appeared with a purse in one hand and a backpack in the other. From the purse she extracted a photo and gave it to Marie. "This is us – see?"

Marie examined the photo and was amazed at the likeness of the two girls. The pair in the cropped picture could have been twins. Two young brunettes were leaning on a third person who was off the photo's cut edge; only an arm with a load of jewelry was visible.

"The two of you could certainly fool me," Marie said. She examined the photo. "You both seem very happy. What caused you to run away?"

"Well – fun, I guess. Jess and I decided to head out on a lark. You know – just to have some fun."

Marie wrinkled her brow and asked, "You ran away for fun?

"We were miserable at school. The photo was taken *after* we left." Brooke sucked in a breath and again looked upward with closed eyes. "Let me explain it this way," she said. "The Paxtons...my parents...they left on a world tour. Her's – Jessie's – they never cared for her in any true sense. The Paxtons – ah – you know – my folks, well they were gone...hard to reach...and ...well..."

She paused, collected her thoughts, and continued. "You see, it was 'us against the world' in our eyes. We had each other and wanted to try to be something big – be something. Yeah – be something different. In the end we wanted to be in New York – Manhattan. But first, we wanted to see the nightspots along the upper part of the shore...on our way to New York. "Things sort of unraveled at a club in Long Branch – a dump named The Sandbar. It's all the way north up the shore, past Asbury Park."

"I know the place. My uncle – the guy who scared you so much a couple of minutes ago. He was sort of famous there, and a lot of other places along the shore. " Marie said with a sprig of pride.

Brooke went blank for a moment of thought then resumed her tale. "Well, it was there – yes – it was there that this sort of Jamaican reggae dude and his gang of girls got us messed up. He said he was singer – talked a lot about his band and the gigs he did – all that sort of stuff. Jessie was taken in by his line, but I was really suspect of his whole act. I didn't like him one bit. And the girls he had hanging on him – they were cheap – all of them were cheap. I didn't trust any of them."

"Tell me about the guy," Marie urged.

"He was a phony – a fake. There's nothing good about him at all. And he was all over Jessie. You know – telling her how hot she was – buying drinks – stuff like that. I told her to ignore him but she didn't listen."

"After a while I went to the restroom, and when I came out everyone was gone. Raff – that's his name – he left with Jessie, and his girls. They were gone, without any goodbyes. Jessie was just gone! I was out of my mind with worry and I was asking the guy running the bar what happened when the police came in. I tired hiding but they got me for under-aged drinking. They could have put me in jail, but I put on a show. I cried, whined – whined and cried. After sitting in a police car for a while being scared silly – they let me go with a warning."

"I asked around and I found out that he was from Atlantic City – that's where I headed. I never found him or Jessie. It was like – like – every time I was close – he just was a step ahead. When I ran out of money I decided to come to Ocean City."

"Did you really think you could hide in the storeroom?" asked Marie.

Brooke grinned shyly and shrugged. "It was worth a try – wasn't it?"

"If nothing else, it took determination."

"I am determined – never to go back to *that school!*" She looked about, waved her hands. "Me being here is like – you know – fate. I walked past one of the shops on Asbury and that's where I saw something – Jessie's jewelry. I was meant to see it. Jessie would never let go of her jewelry. I know that." Brooke clenched both fists and her whole body as she said, "I'm dead set on getting my – I mean Jess's jewelry back. It's important to me!" She grabbed Marie's hand and pleaded, "Please, won't you help me?"

Marie looked long and hard at Brooke, then asked, "What do I do with a runaway whose parents are somewhere on the other side of the globe?"

'YOUR SHIRT IS INSIDE-OUT.'

Joe slid his mug across the counter to signal that he was ready for another *Yuengling* draft. At the end of each day the boatyard's tradesmen and the owners working on their boats congregated in a makeshift bar for a few beers and spirited talk. Joe's celebrity status often made him and his musical past topics of conversation.

Ben, one of the workers, asked, "Joe, we've learned that you know somethin' about boats, but we wanna know what it was that got you into the music business instead of doin' honest work?" The comment drew laughter from all in earshot.

Marie, who had arrived to visit her uncle, was immediately outside the bar. She paused on her way in to listen to her uncle's answer.

I love it when he talks. In person, his voice is even more distinctive than when it comes over the airwaves.

Inside, Joe took a sip of beer and answered the question.

"It never really was a business to me," he began. "If it had been – I sure wouldn't be here scrapping and painting my own boat!" The assembly laughed and then Joe got a bit more serious. "To tell the truth, music wasn't actually what attracted me. I was after something more basic – belonging. In truth, I just wanted to belong." He drained his mug and motioned for another refill. "Let me explain. As a kid I lived in a predominately Italian neighborhood in Philly. My Dad was Greek and Mom was German – definitely not part of the majority on our block of row houses. "Well ..." He sipped his new brew. "... being on the outside – I just wanted in. All the Italian kids were singing on the street corners. They were having such a great time.

And I wanted to be like them. In the beginning, it was as simple as that."

"I was hooked," he continued. "From then on and music became my life. But if I had been Italian, or black, it might have pulled even more. Did you know – Doo Wop came out of both those groups' vocal music roots at their churches? It was in church choirs that they learned to harmonize. Well – if I had been from that tradition – maybe I'd not have craved it like I did from the outside. All of it was exotic to me – the harmonies, the nonsense syllables, the beat, being part of a group – I was crazy for it. I was just a pup when I heard Frankie Lymon and the Teenagers singing *Why Do Fools Fall in Love* and I dreamed, 'if only I could be part of something like that!' I tried when I was a teenager, but my whiskey voice was not really meant to fit in with the perfect vocals performed by the Philly groups I loved."

"Like the Starlighters and the Intruders?" Ben interjected. "*I'm Girl Scoutin'* is my favorite."

"Ben, for a youngster you know your Doo Wop," commented Joe.

"A shame that it died so fast," another worker said in support of the genre.

Joe chimed in, "It lived on and influenced a lot of styles. What we know as the Jersey Shore sound owes its vocal harmonies to Doo Wop. It has even had some notable revivals – like...like...Billy Joel's *For the Longest Time* in '84. That was a worthy tribute. "

"And don't forget Gamble and Huff – they went on writing and producing stuff forever," Ben added.

"Excellent point," Joe said. "They were the masters. They understood what Southside Johnny meant when he said the music 'was aiming for expression not perfection.' Being right is better than being perfect. My voice proves that."

Marie could have listened forever, but decided it was time to enter the bar and share with Joe what she had learned about Brooke. With his back to the door there was no way he could see the person approaching from behind, yet Joe greeted his unannounced guest when she was an arm's reach away. "Hey, little girl. I smelled your perfume and heard your steps – can't be none other than my favorite niece, Marie. I thought you were never leaving Ocean City. What brings you to this end of the causeway? Another mouse hunt?"

"You, Uncle Joe," Marie said, as she thumbed the exposed seam of his shirt. Chiding him, she continued, "Is this how a music legend dresses? Do you realize that you've got your shirt on *inside out!*" She gave him a hug and kissed him on both cheeks.

Joe shrugged. "I dress how I feel. The boat's not cooperating – needs more work than I expected. *And it was vandalized!* Imagine – it's a wreck and somebody broke in."

"Was anything taken?"

"No – and that's the oddest part. Why would anyone hit my old barge when so many nice ones are so close?" He did not wait for an answer. Instead Joe tapped on his shirt. "Well, sweetheart, it's been that kind of day. I dress like I feel – I'm inside out today." He waved for a second mug, and nudged the guy next to him to move down a seat. "Slide down, Kenny – make room for my lovely niece."

Kenny, who had been oblivious to the conversations and people around him, moved silently to the next seat without taking his eyes of his sports page.

"I need to talk to you about our mouse – her name is, Brooke. She's a runaway."

"*Runaway* – big hit for Del Shannon in 1961," Joe said.

Marie smiled and focused Joe back on subject. "Her story prompted me to come see you."

"When I flushed her out I sensed she wasn't just an old

ordinary mouse. That's why I beat a trail here to the marina."

"You're right – she's not ordinary," said Marie.

"Okay. I am all ears. Tell me about her."

"Her family used to own the Atlantic Inn."

"That's why she's been hiding in our storeroom?"

"Yes – it was a safe base for her. She was sleeping there at night and attempting to solve a mystery by day."

"A mystery? I love a good mystery."

"What about a *disappearance or a kidnapping*?"

"Even better – tell me all about *that*."

She scooted her stool closer. "I knew you'd be interested, Uncle Joe – it's a beach thing. She and her best friend, Jessie, ran away from their boarding school and lit out on a road trip up the shore."

"In my day we called them field trips."

"Well, this field trip went bad – real fast. Brooke said she lost track of Jessie up north in a Long Branch club. She believes something terrible happened and can't get any one to investigate."

"Does she have anything solid to go on? Any proof – some sort of lead?"

"Jessie's jewelry – miraculously showing up in the window of a shop right here in Ocean City. Here – take a look." Marie handed him the photo Brooke had shared and pointed. "It's the necklace and bracelet here on Jessie – not all that stuff on the arm of who ever got cut out of the picture."

"This jewelry – the stuff that looks like a mermaid – it got from Long Branch to here? How?

"That's the mystery?"

"And the disappearance that could be a kidnapping?"

"It's part of the mystery, too."

"I think I should talk to your mouse."

THE SAD SONG OF A
SADDER SINGER

Glenda Thornberry pushed an unruly clump of orange-blond hair off her forehead for what seemed like the millionth time. Although it was cold outside perspiration beaded her face and a rivulet of sweat made its way down her neck into her ample cleavage. She had been sitting in the van snorting coke and sipping flavored vodka for quite some time. Glenda was alone and getting worried.

He's been gone way too long, she told herself.

Since departing the hills of East Tennessee three years earlier Glenda's life had spiraled ever downward. Her dream of a country-music singing career died when she reluctantly acknowledged that large breasts and a mediocre voice were not enough to impress the serious talent agents on Nashville's Music Row. Following a string of back-up vocalist gigs with third-rate country-rock bands Glenda had found herself stranded, broke and alone, in New Jersey.

It was on the Atlantic City boardwalk that Glenda's ample bust-line became her most valuable asset for making a buck. She met Raff who was trolling for non-singing talent and the rest is history. Glenda was soon a member of Raff's stable of girls servicing the casinos and nearby hotels. Learning the ways of the oldest profession was easy for Glenda. She also learned how to do drugs; the hardest kind.

Glenda quickly became Raff's favorite. He liked having her drive him about town. The sudden departure of Francine made Glenda's position all the more solid, especially since she knew where Raff stashed his stolen dope and where he hid the mound of cash he had skimmed from his bosses.

Glenda literally knew where the bodies were buried. Raff lusted for Glenda's large breasts so keenly that he had dropped his guard, confided in her, and included her in some of his most dangerous and grisly undertakings.

In the beginning Glenda went along with Raff out of curiosity, and later out of fear. Raff held a tight grip on Glenda because she knew his real identity and the reason why he had burned off his fingerprints. And Glenda knew that he would never let her simply walk away from his control. Too scared to flee and numbed by drugs, her lot in life was eroding daily.

What's taking him so long? She nervously asked herself. *Raff said getting rid of the girl's body would go fast. This ain't like the other times. God, I'm scared. Raff said he'd get help – told me to wait. Damn, I gotta pee, bad!* She fumbled through her purse to examine her cache. *As long as my supply holds out, I'm good*, she thought. *Raff told me to wait*, she reminded herself. *I got to be head bitch by doin' just as I'm told. I better do as told.* She wiggled in the seat. *I'll wait – can't do nothin' else.*

With her eyes closed she relived the recent events that led her to where she sat. The abduction had not gone as planned. The young blonde girl had been completely surprised by Raff's sudden appearance on her jogging path. Getting her into the van was not a problem.

The snatch and grab was quick and both kidnappers were certain the operation went unseen. Their escape plan was simple: Drive south down the beach road; turn right at 8th, and take the Route 72 Causeway. In a few minutes the van was headed east over the causeway and off the island. It was then that things began to unravel.

When they reached the mainland, Glenda gazed at the van's instrument panel and realized they were extremely low on gas. "Raff, we need to get gas. Now!"

"Shit!" he yelled, "do I have to think of everything?"

"I'm sorry, Raff, but I didn't have any money, and ..."

He pointed at the nearest convenience store and yelled, "Pull into the WaWa!"

Raff threw her the wad of money. Some of the bills were from what he had taken off Francine. Glenda had never seen him give up so much, so fast.

"Keep it all," he told her. "Just get us some gas and outta here. Damn! We better not be seen. This is the only God-damned state where you can't fucking pump your own fucking gas." Glenda guided the van to the pumps as told.

An attendant approached the van while Raff covered the girl with a blanket. "Make sure that the only thing this old dude sees is your tits!" He slipped a chloroform-filled rag under the blanket, placing it directly over the girl's mouth and nose. The girl was clearly unconscious, but Raff wanted no problems from her.

When the attendant arrived Glenda rolled down the window and held the bill near her breasts. To her new admirer she said, "Make this regular." The man's eyes ignored the bill and focused on her.

"Is that all?" he asked.

Glenda pushed her chest forward and said, "For now, Honey." She smiled, gave him the bills, making certain to touch his hand. The attendant stumbled twice on his way to the pump. He kept looking back at Glenda and the van.

"Good job," Raff whispered. "The old fart can't keep his eyes off you."

Glenda watched the attendant using the van's side mirror. "Raff, he's staring – and he's creeping me out."

Raff eyed the attendant. "Stay cool. As soon as he's finished get us moving."

The girl groaned and shifted her position under the

blanket. Raff reapplied chloroform to the rag and clamped his hand down harder than before over her mouth and nose. The girl stopped breathing.

Raff lifted the blanket. "Damn!" he yelped. "We got a problem."

"What's happened?"

"We got a big problem! Let's roll – *now!*" he ordered.

At the pump, the attendant was finished fueling, but was still fumbling with the gas cap. Glenda started the engine, put the van in gear, and drove off, leaving the attendant with a surprised look on his face, and the gas cap in his hand.

"Hey!" the startled man cried out, "You –" He waved at the van as it sped into westbound traffic.

"Keep going," instructed Raff.

"Where to?"

"Straight – go straight – just keep going. Get past the Parkway and just keep going."

"What the fuck is happening?"

"We gotta dump this bitch – quick!"

"Why? We just snatched her."

"Because she's dead!"

"Dead!? Wha – wha – what do you mean?" Glenda's voice revealed that she was in unchartered territory and getting scared. "I'm not good with this!"

"Shut the fuck up – let me think!"

"What happened?"

"Had to be too much chloroform. I was trying to make sure she wouldn't cause a fuss at the WaWa. Just keep driving west – I'll tell you where to turn."

Shivering, Glenda did as she was told. "Oh, Jesus! What's happening? What's happening?" The downward spiral she was in accelerated. "Oh my God! Oh my God!"

~ ~ ~

Several miles into the Pinelands National Reserve, a

rear tire on the van blew out just as Raff was telling her to turn off the road. Glenda aimed for a narrow sand-packed trail and fought to keep from hitting the multitude of pines on both sides of the vehicle. She managed to navigate a quarter mile before the flat spun off the rim. Without traction the van sputtered sideways and came to a halt. "We can't go any more," Glenda announced.

"It'll have to do," announced Raff. He opened the sliding door to remove the dead girl from the van. "I'm taking her off a ways – I got to bury her – then I'm walking to the road. I'll phone for help when I get there. You stay with the van."

"No, Raff. No. Why can't we leave it and I go with you?"

"I got product in the van. Can't be walking around with it. Stay here. You're far enough from the road – nobody can see you." Raff heaved the girl's limp body over his shoulder and headed into the pines. "I'll get someone to come for us – just stay put!"

Another hour later, Glenda was at her bursting point. *I don't care what he said, I gotta pee, I gotta pee, I gotta pee!* She grabbed her purse, eased out of the van, and made her way in to the nearby trees to do her business. Just as Glenda dropped her pants she heard a car arrive. Doors opened, and quickly closed. She could hear Raff and someone else. From her squatting position Glenda peeked from behind a pine tree.

Perfect timing, she told herself. *Help comes, and I'm out here – like this!*

"Where's the dead girl?" asked Mr. Someone Else.

"About ten yards in the woods," Raff answered as he pointed.

I know him, Glenda observed, *it's that cop – the one who was always around Francine.* She wiggled to pull her pants up. She remained crouched, wondering, *what's he*

87

doing here?

"Is there any product in the van?" asked the cop.

"Yeah – my girl is watching over it."

"Get it and her out here!"

Raff entered the van. In a moment he appeared with the dope. He held it up for the cop to see.

"Where's your girl?" asked the cop.

"Don't know," Raff said. "She must have headed up the road that goes into the woods – we didn't pass her coming in."

The cop was frustrated. He raised his voice. It quivered as he shouted, "I warned you! Didn't I make things clear? You've got a dead girl in the dirt and a whore witness wandering around in the God-damned woods!"

"Man, I tell you –"

"Shut up!" He pulled a gun and waved it. "Shut the fuck up!"

"Man – don't be trippin' on me. I –"

"Don't say anything else!" The cop pointed the pistol directly at Raff's chest. His voice more cracked as he yelled, "I was never going to do this kind of thing for them. But you fucked up so bad with that little girl – the whole state is looking for this van!"

He fired and Raff fell backward in the roadway. Blood spurted from a hole in the middle of his chest and the sandy soil around him quickly became red.

Glenda froze. Her mind raced.

Oh my God – Oh my God! This is bad – so bad! First, the girl – then, Raff – then...me? Oh shit! He knows I was here!

Glenda slowly eased her way backward.

I have to get deep into these woods!

She inched her way deeper into the Pine Barrens, and as she did, Glenda heard the cop use his phone to report the shooting.

"This is Detective Perry Vale of Atlantic City reporting shots fired – one of the suspects in the LBI kidnapping is down."

Glenda's mind raced more. She did not hear the entire report as she scrambled away. *He said, 'one of the suspects!' Everyone knows I ride with Raff. I've got to get out of here – I've got to disappear!*

GONE HUNTING

Joe gave a nod to Jenny, his favorite server, slid onto his favorite chair in the Sunrise Café, and waved an invitation for Brooke to take a seat opposite him. To the casual observer the pair looked like a father and daughter out for lunch. However, a closer examination would have revealed that Brooke viewed her older male companion as something more. In a very short period of time the two had bonded. Or better said, the runaway girl had attached herself to Joe.

As soon as Marie had told him about "the mystery" Joe had returned and interviewed Brooke at length. From then she had become his shadow at the inn and even helped him with work on the *Summerwind*. Brooke's rebellious and adventuresome nature reminded Joe of his own struggles at that age and he welcomed the opportunity to mentor the girl while learning all he could about her plight.

~ ~ ~

As Brooke took her seat, Joe reflected on what had transpired after capturing the intruder Marie called, The Mouse.

While at the Marina's informal bar Marie had shared what she had learned directly from Brooke's account. She also shared the content of her phone conversation with Sister Juliana, Headmistress for The Sisters of Sorrows School.

From Sister Juliana, Marie learned that Brooke had left school the day after her eighteenth birthday. The school attempted several times to contact her parents, but failed. Because Brooke is of an age where she is free to return to us or not, the Sisters of Sorrow are unable to do much more.

"It's totally up to her," Sister Juliana told Marie. "She needs to come back and remain out of contact with Jessie – but I doubt that she will." The displeasure in the nun's voice when she mentioned Jessie was real. "I've loved all the girls under our care," she said, "but, I must admit that Jessie was the hardest for me. Her parents sacrificed a great deal to send her here – and we waived many costs. But Jessie never seemed to care. She cared only about herself. As an upperclassman she dominated and manipulated Brooke. I did all I could to discourage Jessie from returning to the campus after she had graduated. Off campus I was a failure, and Jessica continued influencing Brooke as soon as she stepped off our grounds. The two of them persisted in their unhealthy relationship and they ran off together. You telling me that one of them has met up with something ill surprises me only in that it is Jessie and not Brooke who is missing. Jessica was the cunning one and we here at the school always thought she would survive in the outside world based on her dark nature."

Marie felt compelled to say something positive; not for Jessica but, rather for the sister's spirits. "Jessie did inspire loyalty." The attempt failed.

"I am saddened to learn that Brooke is still wasting her life on being associated with Jessie. Please tell Brooke that she may return at any time and we will welcome her back. Also, tell her that whether she chooses to come back or not, we will pray for her."

Marie did share the message and Brooke responded by reiterating her determination to reclaim Jessie's jewelry and find out what happened to her friend. Marie then shared everything with Joe and slyly enlisted him into the effort to find out what happened to Jessica.

"She's just a kid," Marie told Joe. "What do we do with her?"

Joe had smiled and recalled his time as a rebel decades ago. "She's obviously not the kind of kid we can *do* anything with – or, *to*."

"Then I should be following your lead on how to treat her?" asked Marie.

"I'd say, 'don't plan to treat her any way at all – just let her be.' "

"That's it?"

"I'd say so. Brooke could be categorized as a troubled kid, but she may be on to something. I'm impressed by her sincerity. You are, too – or else you would have turned her over to the cops, back to the nuns, or called her parents to come get her. You did none of that. In your gut you think she's on the right track."

"I must say, as another female, I trust her burgeoning woman's intuition."

"You would – and should," said Joe. 'Her deep-seated loyalty for a missing friend – the willingness to do something about it – that impressed you. It damn sure impresses me!"

"So what's next?"

"I say we should check out the shop on Asbury."

~ ~ ~

Joe's mind returned to the present.

He liked Brooke and sincerely wanted to help her. After checking out the boutique and getting the same answers he took her to the Sunrise diner for a sit-down. Joe had seen enough at the shop and wanted to ask Brooke some detailed questions.

"I believe you are right," he told Brooke. "That woman in the store is lying. She knows the jewelry is stolen – it was all over her face when I pressed her for details about where they were made. She was playing way too dumb for no good reason. The question is: What else does she know?"

"You *do* believe me." Brooke smiled fully for the first time since Joe and Marie had flushed her from her hiding place in the Atlantic's storeroom.

"I never doubted your story, Brooke."

"Then why did you go to the store to check up on what I told you?" The teenager was very comfortable with Joe and felt that she could question him like a peer. Joe seemed to like the arrangement.

"I had to see things for myself. I wanted to get confirmation," he explained.

"Why – if you never doubted me?"

"It's just the way I am." Joe waved, signaling that they were ready to order.

Jenny approached the table, smiled at Joe, and addressed Brooke. "What will you have?"

Jenny was ready with her pad.

"Tuna melt and a Coke," Brooke said.

Jenny nodded to Joe. "Will it be your usual?" she asked.

"Sure. Why change?"

Jenny confirmed Joe's standard lunch. "BLT, extra crispy bacon, heavy mayo, a cup of today's soup, and unsweetened ice tea, right?" Joe nodded and Jenny disappeared into the kitchen.

With ease Brooke picked up the conversation where it had been interrupted by the ordering of the food. "Tell me what you *really* think about the woman in the shop."

"I *really* think I saw a person get overly defensive when I just asked her a couple of questions."

"Just asked? It's *how* you asked. You certainly have a way of questioning that sends chills up and down my spine. My stepfather has nothing on you. I'd hate to come home late from a date and have you waiting with that voice of yours. Don't you think that *maybe* you just plain scared her?" Again, she felt at ease in addressing him as an equal and even challenging his forceful approach.

Joe knew by Brooke's expression that a friend had arrived. He finished his comment as he eased sideways in the booth. "Fear was exactly the effect I was going for. I want her afraid and nervous – for the next time."

"Next time?" Brooke matched his move and opened a space on her side of the booth.

"Yes, when I go back – alone. That's when I'll really rattle her. Right now, she's wondering if you were just a kid dragging her father or maybe a weird uncle into her shop."

"Speaking of weird uncles," said Marie. She laughed as she slid into the booth.

"You have developed a habit of sneaking up on me," kidded Joe.

"I'm practicing being a stalker. When you revive your music career you will thank me for the publicity I'll generate."

"Now, I know who you are!" Brooke said with excitement and what appeared to be genuine admiration. "You're Jersey Shore Joe!"

Joe suppressed a small blush. "I'm impressed you know my name."

"You were the answer to one of the questions in my music appreciation class," Brooke explained. She addressed both of them with enthusiasm. "The music of the Jersey Shore is a really interesting topic. If all of my classes were that good I'd have studied all the time." She looked at Joe. "Wow! Here you are, Jersey Shore Joe. You're an important cultural celebrity!"

Joe looked to Marie, and said with a grin, "Maybe you were right in calling me a legend."

Brooke continued. She was eager to display her knowledge of music. "We learned that when you performed – you bridged the gap between South Philly

Doo Wop and the developing North Jersey Shore Rock scene. That was in the 1960's. Without Jersey Shore Joe we may not have had The Asbury Jukes, Springsteen, Bon Jovi, and a lot more. Your early work at the Upstage Club was fusion music at its best – that was before there even was fusion music. Some experts believe that it is a great loss that so much of your early work was never recorded."

"Now I am *really* impressed," beamed Joe. "You do know your stuff. But sadly, time has past, and I'm afraid that appreciation for my type of music is fading even faster. In fact, I'm no longer in the music business. And my performing days are even further behind me than radio gigs." Joe smiled slightly and paused. "However, my career is not important. Let me share what is."

Brooke slumped and remained silent.

Joe was visibly touched by her sad look and tried to uplift her spirits. "Brooke, you've really impressed me and Marie. And I am particularly impressed with your spirit – your tenacity – and your loyalty to Jessie. You risked a lot by going it alone and camping out in the Atlantics' storeroom. We believe you and we will help. My visit to the shop is just the beginning."

Brooke sat straight up, blurted, "Thank you! Thank you so much!" and hugged Joe.

A surprised and somewhat embarrassed Joe awkwardly accepted the hug and looked to Marie for relief. "What have you got me into?" he asked.

"Uncle Joe – I think it's being part of a community, a place called home. You know – all the things you like about being here."

As if on cue, Jenny dropped off the orders and asked if she could get anything else.

"I want a drink," Joe said, "but, since the Ocean City is dry, I'll settle for coffee."

The trio of Marie, Jenny, and Brooke laughed. Joe

shook his head in mock despair and muttered, "What am I in for – what am I doing?"

"An adventure," Marie said, "a quest, and a treasure hunt." She instructed Brooke. "Tell us again everything you can remember about the last time you saw Jessica. Tell us about the Rasta Man, his entourage, and the white van."

BANG!

Joey Valentine dropped his pants and planted his considerable bulk onto the toilet seat. The porcelain fixture creaked and groaned beneath his weight. Just as Joey opened the magazine to begin his daily ritual, his phone rang.

"Damn!" he exclaimed, "I can't even take a crap in peace!" Joey glanced at the number on the display and called for his partner. "Hey, Ton – you better take this. It's our little cop friend." He slid the phone under the door with his foot.

A hand reached down. "Jesus, Joey! You pig! Light a match or something! You're stinkin' up the whole building!" Just Tony grabbed the phone. "I'm taking this call outside."

Joey laughed. "I wish I could go with you – 'cause you're right, I really am ripe today."

"Today? Some fuckin' joke!"

Ten minutes later, and several pounds lighter, Joey joined his partner in the poolroom. "What did our little pal want?"

Just Tony told him, "Good news and bad news – which do you want to hear first?"

"You know me, Tony. I always like to take the shot first – then I can enjoy the good stuff. Tell me the bad. I bet it has to do with the eggplant. Right?"

"You got it. Here's the bad stuff – you ain't gettin' that piece of cherry beaver you put on order."

"Damn!" Joey said. "I guess I can live with it, if that's the bad news. The good must be pretty terrific."

"It is. Our young pal nailed that fake Rasta bastard."

"Now *that* is good news! You get any details?"

"Sure. He staged a bust, just as we suggested. Did it out of the city – in the Pine Barrens."

"Good move. It makes sense."

"Imagine that, he wasted the eggplant after all that whining about doin' a hit. Bam – he does it right away!"

"I wonder what changed his attitude."

"That fuckin' idiot Raff messed up on getting you a girl – that's why. He got way too much exposure by trying to snatch one off the street!"

"What!"

"Where have you been?"

"What do you mean? What went down?"

"The idiot grabbed a girl in broad daylight."

"Where?"

"Up on LBI. Somebody saw him and one of those alerts was called. The cop-radio and the media has been alive with it."

"I can't believe it. In broad daylight?"

"I told you he was bad news – that's why we had our little pal watching him and his girls. Francine was going to rat on all of us. It was genius on our part to make sure that who she thought she could squeal to was our guy. Raff knew what cop was safe and Rasta boy called our pal for help when he accidentally snuffed the girl from LBI. He buried the wheels of his van in the sand on some back road. That's when our cop friend decided to do as we told him. *Very* messy, but now clean."

Joey laughed. "Cleaning it up out there in the Pine Barrens is smart. The kid done good."

"Yeah – out in the woods was smart. *And*, he recovered a portion of our product. He used some for cover – gonna play the hero cop. We'll get the rest back – he's bringing it in after he finds that dead creep's woman. More bad news – she's a loose end."

"What's with her?"

"He thinks she knows where more stuff is hidden and where Rasta Boy buried his cash. I'd say we're due for an extra payday. The kid believes he can trace her."

"That's good, Tony. But, taking care of the Rasta boy and his woman isn't the end of our problems. There's still that fat cop, his partner."

"That will come, Joey. It's only a matter of time. We can deal with Klepp later. The bright side of things is that the kid crossed the final line. We own him. We own his ass *and* his soul."

TELL ME A STORY

Joe sipped his second cup of coffee and listened to Brooke's third run-through of the events that led up to Jessie's disappearance. He was impressed by her precise recollections. On each recounting Brooke had not significantly altered her account.

When she finished, Joe waved for another re-fill for his cup, and said, "Your Rasta Man is no musician – that I know. I'd say he's a parasite using the clubs and music scene for selling drugs and pimping. It's a familiar story."

"Wow – you're something," Brooke said with admiration.

"I keep tabs on all the music acts along the Shore," Joe explained. "I know them by their members, music style, instruments, agents, girlfriends, fans – everything. Hell, I even know the make and model of the vans they haul their gear in."

"That's amazing," cooed Brooke.

"Not really," said Joe. "Until recently, I had no life other than music, or more correctly, the music of the Jersey Shore. If it's true that we are all ignorant – just about different subjects – then, it's equally true that we all can be experts about something. My expertise is a narrow field of music, its people, and its related geography."

"As I said, that's exactly why I asked her to tell you everything," said Marie. "We need an expert and you are it. The field does not matter."

"Will a mere *legend* do?" joked Joe. "I'll locate the Rasta Man. It shouldn't be too difficult – I'll make a couple of calls. If he's been attempting to front as a musician anywhere along the shore, I'll find him. At the same time we wait for my feelers to be answered I want to nail down how that jewelry got from way up on the shore to the shop on Asbury. I'll need some time and help on that, but we'll get an answer."

Brooke cheered, "I know you can do it – I just know you can!"

"Don't get your hopes up too high, too soon," cautioned Joe, "and, be prepared to hear messages you don't want to listen to." His tone was more preacher than DJ. "Brooke, you are young – just starting in life. It throws you curves, sinkers and screwballs. Nothing is tossed underhand."

Marie sighed then commented, "A baseball analogy? You must be really in to this, Uncle Joe. No reference to music?"

WHAT HAVE YOU BEEN UP TO?

Although the Internal Affairs Division was off the beaten track and tucked away at the end of a hallway, Detective Big Boy Johnny Klepp avoided the entire third floor as if it was coated with fresh dung. He had been investigated by the division on more than one occasion and hated the very idea of someone policing cops.

If you don't trust cops who can you trust? Klepp thought in his own defense. *Jeez, I hate this place.*

Union representative, Bill Coyle, was waiting for him when he stepped off the elevator. Since leaving the active detective roll, Coyle had become a fixture on the bench immediately outside the Division's door.

"Morning, Johnny," Bill said. "You l...l...look unhappy. Word is you screwed up. Left your...ah...ah...rookie partner – he bags a k...k...kidnapper, ends up a hero, and you remain a zero."

"Fuck you, Bill," Klepp grunted. He took a half-playful half-serious swing at Coyle, aiming for the gut. "Oh, I forgot – Good morning, Officer Coyle. I m...m...meant to s...s...say 'fuck you...ah...ah...*v...v...very m...m...much.*'" Klepp loved to mimic Coyle's stuttering. At times Coyle could control it, but seldom around Klepp, and never when stressed.

Coyle emitted a weak laugh. "You c...c...crack me up, B...Big B...Boy – you get c...c...called in by Internal Affairs, and it's just another day to you. I wish everyone was...ah...ah...ah...as optimistic."

"It's easy when I got friends like you, B...B...Billy B...Boy," Klepp said.

"Friends? Give me a break – at one time or another you've pissed off everyone in Atlantic City, *and* half of New

Jersey." When pissed, Coyle could speak fine.

"Yeah – yeah – yeah," answered Klepp. "Any idea why I am here?"

"None. Could be ah...ah...a background statement on how and why your rookie partner was out of jurisdiction when he brought that kidnapping pervert down. He'll b...b...be on admin leave until the shooting investigation is completed. You'll be s...s...sidelined, too."

"Lovely."

Bill Coyle looked at his watch and said, "We're l...l...late."

"Good – I like making them wait."

"See! It's like I said – you j...j...j...just love to p...p...piss people off."

"I believe it makes me a better cop if I keep an edge."

"Some edge – let's go – I've g...g...got another appointment after this."

"Care to share?"

"No. I c...c...can't."

"Bill, I know I owe you big time – and trust me – I'll make good one day. But I wanna know in advance why I'm here."

"I can't tell you a t...t...t...t...thing."

"Asshole."

"There you go again – now, you're even pissing *me* off". Coyle walked in the direction of the Internal Affairs office. Over his shoulder he said, "Johnny, you're your own worst enemy."

Klepp followed a few paces behind him. Inside the office they were directed into a meeting room occupied by two officers. No introductions were made. Klepp spoke first. He paid no heed to Coyle's instructions, and drew first-blood with a verbal barb aimed at a cop he knew well. "Malone, how's your porn business doing?"

Coyle said, "Johnny, I t...t...told you n...not ..."

Jeff Malone, a long-time IA officer, interrupted. "It's okay, Bill. Considering the source, I expected a lot worse."

"Really?" said Klepp. "Maybe I should start over. I should have been more specific – like – how's your kiddie-porn business?"

"Shit!" barked Coyle. "That's it – I warned you, K...K...Klepp. The union has looked out for you, c...c...coddled you, and smoothed over every wrinkle b...b...because you have made some decent busts. But I'm not going...ah...ah...along with you anymore."

"Like I said, fuck you *very much*!" Klepp extended a middle finger for emphasis.

"Okay, have it your way, *Detective Klepp*. You are on your own." Coyle quickly left the room without looking back.

Klepp reached over and slammed the door shut behind the departed Coyle. "That went nice," Klepp said to Malone. "I guess I really did piss him off. Him putting a sentence together and calling me Detective Klepp without a stutter proves it." He looked at Malone's silent companion. "And who, may I ask, are you? I know every badge in town and you are a ringer if I ever saw one."

"I'm Rich Kona," the man calmly answered.

Klepp broke into laughter. He bent over and it took him several moments to stop. "I'm sorry – I'm so sorry," he apologized. "Besides being an obvious outsider. I think your name is really fuckin' funny. Man where are you from?"

Kona ignored the question and stared at Klepp.

Klepp responded with a serious looking posture. He moved an imaginary microphone to his mouth and imitated an in-store commercial announcement. "Yes – now found on the coffee aisle – the finest brand made from the richest beans from the hillsides of the Hawaiian Islands – Rich Kona!" He laughed again and pointed at the target of his joke. "I bet they think you're something special at Dunkin Donuts!"

Kona looked to Malone. "Is he for real?"

Malone said to Kona, "It's sad but true." He turned back to Klepp. "You seem to bring the best out in people. That I have to give you."

"It's a gift – I'm glad to share it." Klepp waved his arms around the interview room. "So, why did you assholes drag me in this time? Was it just to meet the Coffee Man?"

Malone said, "If you want, we can reschedule. Rules say you should have a union rep with you."

"Fuck it. Fuck him. And *fuck you!*"

"I take it by that – you do wish to proceed."

"No I *wish* I was rich and had a bigger cock. But go ahead – I'm ready."

"Have it your way," answered Malone. He reached toward a recorder, pushed a key, and said, "It's off, John. We'll make this informal – off the record. You okay with that?"

"Wait a second. I'm supposed to believe you are cutting me a break?"

"Call it what you like."

"My memory tells me what I should call it. It's bullshit."

"I'm just trying to do my job."

"Really? You could've fooled me."

"I just call 'em the way I see 'em."

"Meaning?"

"You may have been a bit rough in the handling of some of your collars. And, you got a little trigger-happy more than once. But, you've come up clean as far as graft is concerned. Klepp, I respect you – in an odd kind of way.
"

"That, I find hard to believe, Malone."

"Believe what you want. But this time we're not interested in you."

"So...why the summons?"

"We need your help. We want you to co-operate with us."

"What? Are you guys crazy?"

Malone answered calmly, "No, we just want you to help check out your partner."

"I knew it! The shooting is a bad one, right?"

Malone looked like he had stepped on a landmine. Kona had a matching expression. No one said anything for several long moments. Each side eyed the other. Finally Malone's new partner broke the silence.

"Are you confused? Do you think Mary Clamson shot someone?" asked Kona.

"What?" asked Klepp. "Clammy? No – no! I'm talking about the kid – Vale. You know *my partner*. He *executed* some no name punk up in the Pine Barrens. That's why I'm here, right?"

Neither man responded. The paused prompted more from Klepp.

"The kid's not right," Klepp insisted. "I know it. He's into something – been lying to me all along. This is about him, right?"

Jeff Malone said, "No, this was *supposed* to be about your *ex-partner*, Mary Clamson. But I think you just brought in a bonus."

"What?"

"We've had Clamson under surveillance for months. She's been busy since you broke up – linked by some reliable intelligence to some potentially nasty stuff."

"How so?" Klepp became somewhat serious.

"Dating an odd grab bag of characters – an Assistant DA, a casino exec, several police officers, and a known criminal figure. Your visit to her office was recorded. We have a tap on all her calls, too."

"Is an active social life a crime?"

"No, but she may be a risk to the department. We watch for abnormalities."

"Abnormalities? Don't come down on her just 'cause she and I once had a fling and then out of deep emotional pain the poor woman dates the known world to get over me."

Klepp's attempt at humor bombed.

"I'd rather we not go into Clamson's thing yet," said Malone. He paused and briefly looked the file before him. "I think this can wait."

"For what?" probed Klepp.

"A lost shipment of black tar heroin that was headed here."

"Clammy? You can't believe she's ..."

Malone shrugged ever so slightly. He looked to his companion for assistance.

Kona stepped in and flipped the file closed. "Later ..." He started the recorder and continued, "I'd like to shift gears. You called Vale's shooting an execution. Would you care to tell us why you used that term?" Kona was now in charge.

Klepp nodded and said, "Sure – like I said – he's a phony. The boy's been jivin' me since day one."

"So?" Kona asked. "Everyone shades the truth – especially the rookie detectives working with older guys like you – they want to fit in. They embellish."

"Not like this guy. Not for crap that doesn't count. Plus, he was running his own investigation without sharing any of it with me. I was his partner and didn't know what he was doing. And he had no interest in what I was doing, except maybe to cover his tracks. I'm telling you – my gut sez that shooting had to be bogus."

Kona replied. "That doesn't sound like you, Klepp –

ratting on a fellow officer – your partner no less."

"Seems like you were counting on it. After all you did want me to snoop on Clammy."

Malone commented. "Her involvement is speculative."

"But solid enough to haul me in here."

"I guess you are right. But why are you so down on your *new* partner?" asked Kona.

"Simple – lie to me and you ain't my partner. Especially if you take down a perp, grab some glory, get placed on admin leave, and still not call me."

"I'd say you weren't close."

"Real funny."

"Let's back up. The word you used was, 'execution.' Care to explain?"

"Whatever Vale's story is – it has to be a joke. The scumbag he shot was a first-class wuss – beating on women was his routine. He never carried a weapon more dangerous than his fists. For some reason he stayed away from guns – maybe had a bad experience with one. Any way – Vale's a liar. But why should you, or I, care? One less creep on the streets is okay by me. Now tell me – why are you so interested?"

Malone said, "We are interested in a lot of things."

"Your fishing paid off," Klepp eyed both IA representatives and grinned. "Looks like now you have an interest in both of my partners. And me opening my big mouth is about to end...unless I get some answers from you fast."

Malone re-opened the file before him. He thumbed through the papers, slid a page toward Klepp and said, "You're right – take a peek."

The veteran detective looked at the page closely. Klepp read the phone call's transcript several times and finally said, "This is what happened just after I left her office, right?"

"Yes."

"Care to tell me who she was talking to?"

"She assigned Vale to be my partner?"

"Sorry, but that's under wraps."

Klepp handed the paper back. "I'll be damned. Looks like I might have two dirty partners – maybe working together?"

"It appears that something like that could be a reality."

"So, what exactly do you want from me?"

Kona pulled in a breath held it for a moment, then said, "John, you were right I am a ringer – here on assignment from DEA."

"Figured something like that – you think Clammy is in drugs? The heroin you mentioned?"

"We don't know. In fact we don't know much for certain. All we know is that a shipment of some black tar heroin is headed here."

"Black tar – that's a game changer."

"That is why we called you in."

"Why me?"

"Like I said, we want you to work for us...full-time."

Klepp was stunned. He looked at his former adversaries and asked, "Did the world just end or something?"

"No," answered Malone.

"You have got to be kidding. Me? In IA – working with DEA?"

"You are the last person anyone would suspect of investigating other cops. But, there you were – in Mary Clamson's office breaking all sorts of rules to investigate another cop. You were following your instincts. We trust that."

"So – you *are* serious. You do want me!"

"Klepp, you may be a total screw-up as a human being, but you *are* one very special natural born investigator.

What do you say?"

"Can I say, 'no'?"

"Not really."

"Crap."

"It's settled," answered Malone. "Welcome to Internal Affairs."

"... and unofficially, the DEA," added Kona.

THE PICKUP

Glenda adjusted the front of her blouse, arched her back, and aimed her chest at the approaching pickup truck. *This should work,* she told herself. After a night hiding in the pines she was back on the paved highway headed toward the shore.

I may look a little rough after wandering all night through those fuckin' woods, she thought, *but I've got the right equipment to stop any one of these local boys. Puppies like mine never fail – they always get rides.*

She was right. The truck pulled over.

A squinty-eyed loner in his late-twenties rolled down the window, grinned, zeroed in on her cleavage, and asked, "Do you need a ride?"

Glenda was quick with a smile and answered, "Sure do, Honey."

Without hesitation she jumped into the cab and slid close to the surprised driver.

"Wh – wh – where to?" the guy asked with more than a tinge of excitement. His eyes were still on her breasts.

Glenda placed a hand on his leg and rubbed while she cooed, "*Anywhere* you want, Honey, anywhere you want." He was putty in her hands. "You got a place we can be alone?" she tempted.

The guy stuttered, "Su – su – sure!" hurriedly put the vehicle in drive and swerved on to the highway.

"Take it easy, cowboy," she told him. "Keep your eyes on the road and at least one hand on the wheel. Just get us safely to wherever it is we are headed."

Glenda was in total control.

"What's your name? I can't keep callin' you, Honey."

"Jeff...uh...Breen – I'm Jeff Breen."

Well, Jeffie, *Honey*, I think we are going to be friends." She flipped open the glove box and rummaged through its contents. Not finding anything of interest, she asked, "You got anything to drink? I mean booze – not soda, or God forbid, water."

"No. But I know where we can get some." He was eager as a puppy.

"How fast is fast?"

"Real fast. I can do it quick if I stop at the liquor store...by...by... my place."

Glenda squeezed his leg again, let her hand drift into his lap, and said, "Liquor and your place. That's perfect!" Jeff's reaction was to press down on the accelerator. Glenda pressed down more and the truck zoomed.

This is easy, Glenda thought. *I'll party a little to get this sorry-assed loser do whatever I want, and use him. I know where Raff's money and dope is hidden. All I have to do is lie low and let everyone forget about me. Then I'll...I'll...I'll what?*

She strained against the spiral that was her life.

Pick up where I left off. That's what I'll do. With some money I can put Raff and all this behind me. Maybe I can be a singer again!

HONOR AMONG THIEVES

Erskine Detwilder, VP for Special Projects, Media Relations, and Community Affairs for Consolidated Entertainment International, Inc., did not like what he saw. He turned off the newscast and angrily tossed the TV remote onto the coffee table. He barked to his companion, "None of this is good. I want to know how you intend to minimize this situation's repercussions!"

Detwilder eyed his subordinate accomplice. *He's become a liability!" Yes, he's become a liability,* he told himself. *I'll distract him with some assignments, and consider how best to deal with him.*

"Minimize?" His underling asked. "Re...re...reperc... c...c...cussions? What do you m...m...m...mean? There's not the slightest h...h...hint in any of the c...c...coverage that the d...d ...d...dead kidnapper is tied to us." *He's going soft – maybe lost it.*

"I disagree. Detective Vale – remember he's a Valentine." *Incompetent fool.*

"But no one outside our inner c...c...circle knows who he really is." *Old fool – can't remember shit.*

"Are you sure? Enough to wager all we have accomplished? Sooner or later someone will ask questions. Someone will ask questions – like, 'Why was he in the Pine Barrens?' 'How did he find the kidnapper?' Trust me – that slob partner of Vale's isn't as stupid as he looks.

"You m...m...may be right." *Lucky is more like it.*

"Damn right – I'm right! It won't take much for someone to learn that the kidnapper is tied to those two thugs pretending to be the cast of some cheap mob movie. They've fouled up everything with their outdated methods. And God! The way they look!" *And you linked them to us through Vale.*

"C...c...certainly a problem." *After all – they work for you, genius!*

"Ask yourself, 'Why on earth would that joke of a musician be on LBI nabbing a child?' The answer will lead to those two idiots – trust me!" *You idiot!*

"So, w...w...what d...d...do we d...do? *Duh!*

"We do nothing! You clean up!"

"S...s...sure."

"Look – our business is terrible and it's not going to improve. We are under assault. Practically every state in the Union is hopping on the gambling wagon – amateurs using the Internet have cut into the sex trade – kids are selling dope – every income stream we have is hurting." He sighed. "It's been decided that we change. Designer sex, gambling, drugs – casino-based vice – our businesses are not as profitable as they were in the past. And remember business is all about money."

"N...n...nothing more?"

"Control – money and control – that's it!" He paused. "But I'm not here to teach – I'm here to wrap things up. It's time to move on. First we clean things up by severing all ties and links." *I'll bail out and leave him holding the bag.*

"M...m...meaning?" *He's going to dump me – I know it!*

"Some people disappear." *Happens all the time to idiots like him.*

"Who?" *What insanity! You can't wave a wand and simply have everything vanish. I'm vulnerable if left behind.*

"The visible ones. We'll daisy chain the work – get our accomplices to destroy each other in sequence and then you'll have just one or two in the end to take care of." *One simple task – and I'm gone.*

"I've arranged for some n...n...nasty happenings in the past but I won't do what you are asking!" *He hasn't the balls to do any dirty work – wants me to do it – and, take the heat if it fails.*

"Who's asking? I'm just stating the obvious. It's time tie up loose ends." *'Bye 'bye and adios!*

"You make it s...s...sound so easy." *He's whacko – I knew he'd fold one day. It's a good thing that I prepared a back-up plan expecting this.*

"It is – all we have to do is keep our heads and stick together." *Until I drop you.*

"Sure – sure – we s...s...stick together." *My next step is to find a way out – find some scapegoats – muddy the waters.*

"That's good! I'm so glad we see eye to eye." *You stupid asshole!*

WHO'S ON FIRST?

Perry Vale gnawed on his fingernails and fretted over being summoned to the dreaded third floor of Police Headquarters.

Shit! I'm in way too deep in this damned mess.

He worried as he waited for the union rep to meet him.

My explanation of how I "stumbled upon" the girl's kidnapper is weak – but I've got to stick to my story. Whatever happens – whoever asks – I've got to remember that I am a suspect in the eyes of Internal Affairs. Stick to your story – just as you've told it – no variations! Variations – that's what the interrogators will look for – variations in my story will ruin me.

"You're h...here early," remarked Bill Coyle. "It's your...ah...ah...first t...t...time, right?"

Vale fidgeted. "Yeah – yeah – my first."

Coyle plopped on the bench sitting close to the anxious rookie. "Re...relax. You b...being here is j...just standard p...procedure." He pulled a file out of his briefcase. "Let's go over ah...ah...a couple of t...t...things before going in."

"Go over? I thought –"

"Don't think!" interrupted Coyle. When preaching about his job he seldom stuttered. "Do not think. Just answer their questions. If you think – they'll get suspicious. If you are telling the truth there is no need to think. Trust me – thinking just screws things up." He looked at his watch and said, "No time to talk – it's time to go."

"But – but – but –" Vale was rattled. "I'm supposed to be a hero. This doesn't make any sense. What if – if – I –"

"What are you w...w...worried about?"

Vale said nothing.

"Good! We're due. N...n...now – let's go. And remember – absolutely n...n...no thinking!"

Inside the office they were met by Malone and Kona. Pleasantries were quickly exchanged. Malone lay back and let Kona run the show. Kona engaged the recorder and recited the standard information of date, attendees, and purpose of the meeting. Then he began.

"Detective Vale, in your report...the *official* report...your *sworn* report..."

Coyle strategically yawned. Vale anxiously shifted his position. Malone watched.

Kona continued. "... in which you explain your presence at the shooting scene as a...a ..." He paused and stared at his target.

Vale squirmed. *What's he doing? Why is he staring at me? What's he driving at? What does he want?*

Kona dragged out the moment. "... a...a...lucky...break. Yes...a...luuuckyyy...break." He continued to stare. "Care to elaborate, Detective Vale?"

Vale began to perspire. His mind went into overdrive.

Let me think – what is he hinting at? Why is he still gawking at me? Why is the other guy – Malone--why is he so quiet? Why is Coyle just sitting there? He's the union rep! Isn't he supposed to protect me? Damn! He told me not to think. Just answer the question. Stick with your story. No variations. Let me think – no – Coyle said not to think!

Damn! thought Coyle. *He's taking too long. I told him not to think about his answers!*

He's hiding something, observed Malone. *He's thinking about his answer – taking too long. He's thinking. He should have spit his answer out immediately.*

Vale finally spoke. "I...I...ah...I...was driving to Philly, and I –"

Kona quickly interrupted, "Philly? You were headed to Philly?"

"Yes – I –"

"That's odd – you don't get to Philly from here by taking Route 72."

Vale froze. His discomfort was visible. He paused in answering.

He's thinking again, thought Malone.

Finally, Vale spoke. "I...I...was...I've got a friend...a girlfriend in Ship Bottom. I left for Philly from there."

"Okay...okay," said Kona. "So...you are headed to Philly...and...and...you come across the suspect *and* the van...a couple hundred yards off Route 72...up what is not much more than a dirt road? I'd say that's more than a *lucky break*. Sounds more like a *miracle*."

"No – no!" Vale exclaimed. "I saw him on the road – on Route 72. I recognized him...from the alert."

"So...he flagged you down?"

"No – no – he was just heading up the turn-off...to where the van was located."

"You say you recognized him ..."

"Yeah – like I said – from the alert."

"So...you never ran across him...here...in Atlantic City...in the course of your duties, right?" Kona asked.

"Right." *Good! I answered quickly – no thinking.*

"What happened next?"

"I...ah...I parked up Route 72 and walked back and followed him up the dirt road."

"Why on foot?"

"I was responding to the alert – being careful, so I parked, and followed him up the dirt road."

"You already said that."

"Did I?"

"You did."

Kona stared. Vale perspired. Malone watched.

After some time, Coyle spoke. "Is that it? Ah... ah...all you want to know is h...how h...he got to the s...s...site?"

"No," answered Kona. "There's the gun." He stared more.

Vale fidgeted and perspired more. "Wha...wha...what about it?"

"When and how did he show the weapon? Tell us about the confrontation."

Vale stopped fidgeting and froze. Again, his mind went into gear. *They suspect something – that's obvious. But what? I have to think. NO! I can't! Oh shit!*

Vale looked to Coyle for help. He stared at the union rep like an actor wanting a prompt for a lost line. Coyle was no help. He stared vacantly back at Vale and then shrugged.

Vale swallowed hard and finally spoke. "Ah...I...ah...I...well...I followed him."

"So we've heard," quipped Kona.

"Yeah – yeah – I know I already said that. I followed him – yeah that's what I did."

"And?"

"I think he heard me – he turned around real fast. That's when I saw the gun."

"So you fired in a defensive mode?"

"Yeah – I fired because he had drawn his weapon. I was –"

"Okay – that's enough," interrupted Malone. "I think we've got all we need for now. Let me recap – you spotted a suspect described in an alert, approached him on foot, and fired in self-defense – right?"

"Yes – that's right!" Vale said quickly.

Malone responded. 'Like I said – that's enough – *for now*." He nodded to Kona.

Kona nodded back. "If we need anything we'll pull you

off admin duty. But I don't expect we'll need to."

"Really?" chirped Vale. He sounded like a truant being let out of detention.

Coyle headed for the door, Vale followed obediently. Outside, he asked, "How'd I do?"

"I've s...s...seen worse – but I c...c...can't remember when, " Coyle said. He turned and walked toward the elevator.

"Aw, come on – tell me. It wasn't that bad – was it?" Vale asked.

Coyle grunted something unintelligible and kept walking.

Vale fretted. *Gotta think – gotta think! Glenda is out there somewhere. If she ties me to the Rasta Man in any way before the shooting I'm toast. I need to find her and silence her. But how do I find her? The money! I tagged the money! If Francine gave any to Raff and he gave some Glenda ...*

~ ~ ~

Malone and Kona waited for Johnny Klepp to join them from his listening post in the adjoining office. "What's your read, Klepp?" Malone asked.

"I told you – the kid's a liar." Klepp plopped in a chair and continued. "Three points hang the little bastard. First, he hasn't got a girlfriend in Ship Bottom, Philly, or on the moon. He's bitched to me more than once about being married to his job with no time for chasing pussy. Second, he knew the suspect – that phony Jamaican, who we now find has sanded his finger tips. That phony island scum sucker has been in our sights for quite a while – we have been tailing him and his crew of street whores for weeks. All that crap about "the kidnapping suspect A" was just that – crap! And finally, third, that sleaze he drilled would never pull a gun. For some reason he had an aversion to going bang-bang. Since arriving on the local scene the

Rasta Man was never known to carry anything. If by some weird chance he ever did have a gun, tell me — what kind of desperado in the drug biz carries a piss-ant .22 caliber automatic? Shit! Talk about a planted throw-down weapon! Only a rookie would try something as lame as that. I told you — this shooting isn't clean." Before Malone or Kona could respond, Klepp added, "Oh yeah — I left out the best part — numero four. The tits!"

"Tits?" asked Kona. He gave Malone a 'there he goes again' look.

"Yeah — big ones," said Klepp, "hanging on Rasta Man's tramp companion, Glenda. Vale neglected to mention him knowing that the white van found at the site of his heroic gun fight *has never* been seen without Glenda and her big tits behind the wheel!"

"So, we may have an accomplice in the kidnapping?" Kona said.

"Better," replied Klepp, "I bet we have a witness to an execution." He made for the door.

"Hey," Malone asked, "where you going?"

"If I'm drafted to play on this team," said Klepp, "then, I plan to enjoy myself. I'm going on a titty run. I'm gonna find Glenda and nail that lying little prick partner of mine. No — correction — my ex-partner!"

When Klepp was gone Kona said, "He's holding something back."

"Why do you say that?"

"Seems like he was in too much of a hurry. Do you think we can trust him not to screw up?"

"Not really. Besides, what other option do we have?"

Kona responded, "Okay, we let the mad dog run. If he tries something, we'll be right behind him...and if he pisses on the tree, we don't know his name."

"Fine by me," Malone agreed, "fine by me."

HELLO!

Marie looked over Joe's shoulder with obvious curiosity and asked, "What's the secret weapon?"

Joe smiled. "No secret – it's just a cell phone."

"Cell phone? You hate cell phones, Uncle Joe. You told me you never owned one and never would."

"Well, I do now. As a matter of fact I have two."

"Two?"

"Yes. I need two for my little project to work."

Joe dialed and Marie looked on in wonder. After he answered his second phone, Joe handed it to Marie, and said, "Stay glued to this." Joe then headed for the consignment shop telling her to "Stay put somewhere down the street. This won't take long."

When Joe reached the shop, he entered and headed straight for Lil.

Lil's face told all. She knew that Joe was back to ask about the jewelry. Lil tried to head toward the stockroom. Joe followed. Along the way to the rear of the store, he hid Phone Number One on a shelf. Lil did not see the move.

At the back of the store Joe caught up with her, and before Lil could speak, he began his assault.

"I need some information. I was in here a while ago with a young girl looking at some jewelry – some mermaid jewelry," he said. "I need to know where it came from."

"I'm afraid I can't say. I'm just the retailer and I –"

"Look! I don't care what story you want to spin – all I want to know is who gave it to you!"

"I – I – I – can't – I – ah –"

"That's not good enough." Joe stared at her.

"I can't say – really. It came as part of a large shipment and – I – I – I"

"Okay, lady, have it your way. Stick to your tale about not knowing anything." Joe spun about and headed for the exit. Over his shoulder he shouted, "But be prepared for my return – with the police!" He slammed the door.

Outside, Joe walked around the corner and called out to Marie. "Do we have anything on Phone Number Two?"

"She's calling someone now—give me a sec." Marie listened. to the open line on the phone Joe had abandoned in the shop.

Inside Lil frantically told Joey Valentine about her visitor. "Joey, a guy was here *twice* – asking about those mermaid items. He knows something, I know it, and I'm scared. He threatened to bring in the cops!"

"Shut up! Get rid of the stuff – fast. Ditch it!" Joey told her, then he changed his mind. "No, no, don't get rid of it. Bring it to me in AC. Bring it right away. And, I do mean, *now*. Do it before anyone comes back to your place!" He ended the call without waiting to hear a reply.

"Oh no!" cried Lil, "No, no, no!" She hurriedly went about closing the shop.

Marie listened until there was no more information to be gleaned. "I'd say she got bad news," she told Joe. "It sounds like she's planning to go somewhere."

Joe grabbed the phone, listened to Lil making a commotion, and then instructed Marie on their next move. "Get your car and follow her. Don't do anything, just follow her. When she meets up with whoever she called, call me." He took Phone Number Two and gave her a slip of paper. "Here's the number for this phone." He stared at his niece and said, "Remember, I don't want you doing anything other than following that woman. Maybe you should take Brooke along."

Marie took the slip and asked, "Where will you be?"

"I'm going back to AC myself."

"What's there for you, Uncle Joe?

"A friend of mine; I think it's time we get some professional help."

FOLLOW THE YELLOW BRICK ROAD

It only took a few calls for Joe to get a line on Raff. The phony Jamaican bandleader's death at the hands of a rookie cop had traveled through the Jersey Shore music community faster than the news of an open gig. Although dead, Raff's end was not the end. Joe had a lead and it was in AC, the same location as his professional friend.

Folks are certainly not bent over in grief because he got shot, Joe observed. It could have been a dead end, but he had a female companion that was pretty much his shadow. I need to find her. But if I'm going to locate her it will require help – and I'll need more clout than an old record jockey can muster. It certainly time for me to call on an old friend.

Joe parked his beat-up truck in front of the Atlantic City Police headquarters and waited for his friend to exit the building.

"Hey Joe!" shouted Johnny Klepp.

The veteran cop bounded out the main door of the police station and straight for Joe. "It's been ages since I last heard from you. People thought I was lying when I told 'em I knew Jersey Shore Joe. Where the hell have you been hiding?"

Before he could answer the surprised DJ was swept along by the big detective. Klepp kept talking as they walked. "What's it been – five – no, six years?" he asked.

"Longer, I think," Joe said.

"I heard you every so often on the radio – always a new station – oddball time slots. Hell, I mostly caught you on night shifts, during stakeouts. " Klepp's eyes were

129

elsewhere as he hurriedly added, "Joe, I need a favor, too. " He had spotted Vale leaving the parking lot.

"Yeah, yeah, no problem," answered Joe. "If you want me to drive you somewhere I can fill you in on why I'm here and –"

"Sure, sure, let's roll," said the big cop, pointing at Vale's car. "Follow that guy right there. But, stay back a bit. I don't want to tip him off." Joe wheeled into traffic a few cars behind Vale.

Once underway, Klepp focused on his friend. "So, what's your trouble, Joe?" he asked. "If ever I've seen a guy looking for help – it's you."

"You've always had the knack, Johnny. You're good at reading people. It made you a great cop. That's why I'm here. I need a cop."

Klepp chuckled. "Like you said, I'm a great one. What's up?"

"I need help finding someone in particular."

"Missing person?"

"Yes, I'm looking for a woman."

"Ain't we all?" Klepp laughed. "Ain't we all!"

"No, it's not like that. I need help finding a *particular* woman. One that has been running with a musician; the one that just got killed in the Pine Barrens."

"The phony Jamaican."

"Yes. That's him. How'd you guess?"

"I am a great cop, remember." Klepp said. "Looks as if we're chasing the same thing, or I mean the same person – Glenda."

"Glenda – that's her name!"

"What's your business with that piece of work?"

"I think she may be the link in finding a girl from Ocean City that has gone missing."

Joe told Klepp all about Brooke and Jessie's adventure, Jessie's disappearance, and the jewelry. He explained about the lead he was given and was about to produce the photo of the girls when Klepp interrupted with directions.

"Ease off the gas and let him stretch it out a little."

Joe did as told and forgot the photo. He resumed the conversation with Glenda as the topic. "Now, this Glenda is my only solid lead. I'm hoping that she or the jewelry will produce something. It's fate that you want to find her, too. Tell me, Johnny – why are you interested in her?"

"She's in the middle of something big – that's all I can say."

"Could it have anything to do with my missing girl?"

"Maybe – maybe not. This is a drugs and hookers thing and – wait a minute!" Klepp went silent for a moment. Then he said, "Maybe it could have something to do with the abduction attempt, or maybe it could be nothing. Lately things have gotten so screwy that ..." Klepp pointed at Vale's car, "You can goose it up some. Don't let him get away."

"How does he fit in?"

"I don't know exactly. But I'm sure he's looking for Glenda, too. He's recently paid a lot of attention to the people she ran with. I say we let him do the heavy lifting."

"Who exactly is it that we are tailing?"

"The guy who shot and killed the phony Jamaican."

"But, wasn't that done by the police?"

"Yeah, but what's that got to do with anything?"

"I'm like most people. I believe that you guys are the good guys."

"Some of us are, some aren't. It's the dope and the piles and piles of money, Joe. The money drives people crazy. Sometimes it's hard to tell who is on which side."

The big detective's voice drifted away for a moment as he fought hard to grab a phantom thought that slipped across the back of his mind and into a memory crevice.

Something is wrong, this ain't right – following Vale right out of Internal Affairs is too easy. They said something about a lost drug shipment – Clammy...nah! It's Vale – that's what I gotta stay focused on.

He said to Joe, "It's easy to be fooled. The stuff right in front of you, the stuff you take for granted, it's the bear that can eat you. It's what eats your soul without you ever suspecting that you are on the menu."

"What are you saying?"

"People want to be deceived. They willingly buy into the obvious. All they desire is to go with the flow. For most, life is just a pleasant illusion."

"Johnny, I never took you for being such a philosopher."

"Comes with age...and being deceived." He pointed ahead at Vale's vehicle. "Just don't lose that car."

"I'm on it." Joe kept at least two cars between them and Vale. "Let me get this right. The guy we are following is your partner?"

"*Was* my partner."

"And you think he's looking for the Jamaican's girl – Glenda?"

"Yes, he has to be. That fake Jamaican would never have been driving around without her. I figure that when my weasel of an ex-partner nailed that creep he failed to take care of the witness. Somehow Glenda slipped away."

"You think that it was an execution – by a cop?"

"I can't tell you all that's going down. But since you are my wheelman, I'll share that I suspected that the guy was bogus from the start. I felt it in my bones."

"So, what's our plan?"

"We tail him. If he finds her we step in."

"And you'll let me talk to her?"

"Sure, why not? I'll make you a deputy, just like in the movies."

"Is that legal? Can you do that?"

"I do whatever it takes."

"But...is it legal?"

"Raise your hand."

"What?"

Klepp motioned. "Your right hand – get it up."

Joe clutched the wheel with his left hand and held up his right.

"Do you solemnly swear –" He stopped. "Nah, that isn't right. Do you promise to love, honor and –"

Joe cracked up laughing, the car swerved, and he grabbed the wheel with both hands. "Johnny, you're nuts, absolutely nuts!"

"Look, when we find Glenda, I'll make sure you get a chance to grill her some and find out what she knows about your missing girl. Legal or not, you'll get a shot at asking her some questions"

"Thanks, Johnny. I need to find out what happened."

"Sure, but don't expect much. That troupe of misfits saw a lot of girls come and go. Glenda may not know what you want. She may know nothing."

"It's all I have to go on. My niece and her friends are on the track of the missing girl's jewelry. Maybe we'll get lucky."

"From what I know about kids, especially runaways, I'd say the girl you are looking for is long gone. She's in Oz."

"Oz?"

"Emerald City, The Land of Oz. You know, that dream place all kids run toward, New York City, Vegas, California, whatever is their version of paradise. She's in Oz, or she's dead."

"You make it sound simple."

"It's either, or."

"Why so simple...and cruel?"

"I've been dogging that Reggae-Jamaican-phony for a while. My eye has been on him and his stable of whores. Besides the usual he's been tied into high-level parties and some missing women. The little girl you're looking for either left him quick or met with a bad end. What else explains the trinkets ending up in Ocean City?"

"I can see a young girl hocking her prized jewelry and skipping town. I hope it's what happened."

"Yeah – it's possible – just possible."

"You sound pessimistic."

"Have to be – I'm a cop – and an old one. I've seen a lot."

"But not my missing girl." He reached for his pocket. "I've got a photo..."

Klepp waved him off and pointed ahead again. "I'll examine it later. Right now, our best bet is to tail my ex-partner and see if he leads us to Glenda."

"I'm on him."

"He's in a hurry – don't lose him. Either he'll lead us to the girl, or to someone who can – like Glenda."

WHERE DEVILS MEET

Marie parked the car, ignored Joe's advice, and told Brooke, "I'm going inside. Just wait for me." She walked across the lot and entered Zebo's Bar and Grille, one of Atlantic City's most popular eating and drinking establishments. Inside she took a seat at the bar, and eyed her target.

That's interesting. Marie told herself as she watched Lil address a grotesquely fat man seated in the midst of several thinner, younger versions of himself. *Fat, over-the-top with attitude, and dressed like a spot-on caricature of a New Jersey thug. He's even finished off with a slight glaze of grease and sweat like he's a product from central casting.*

Marie winced at the image projected by the group. *It seems that tubby and his pals are in love with the gangsters portrayed on TV. They look like re-treads from a bad DVD. Every thinking person in the state is sick beyond measure of the negative images America routinely gets fed about their home.*

`The big man waved to Lil and by his motions ordered that she be seated. As she sat, a slightly older, slimmer, and more sinister man took the seat at the table's head.

They obviously aren't insurance salesmen meeting after work. I need to schmooze the bartender — see what information I can get on Fatso and his friends."

Marie waved the barman over. As he approached she read his nametag and when he arrived Marie slid a twenty across the bar in his direction. "Here, Ted," she said, "this is yours."

Ted eyed the bill and asked, "Why?"

She curled her finger for him to come closer. "Because

you are going to tell me something and then immediately forget about it and me. Okay?"

He picked up the money and said, "Sure. What do you need to know?"

~ ~ ~

A few minutes later outside, Marie headed across the parking lot. She did not see the oncoming vehicle and was nearly hit by the fast moving auto entering a vacant spot. Jumping out of the way she yelled, "Hey – watch it!"

"Sorry – sorry!" yelled the rattled driver. "I didn't see you – I'm really sorry!" Without waiting for a reply Perry Vale exited his auto and sprinted toward the restaurant's entrance.

"Thanks, a lot!" she yelled at the disappearing figure.

Marie walked to the rear of the just parked car and was about to take note of its license when she heard a familiar voice come from a second vehicle just entering the lot.

"Marie!" called Joe. He was at the wheel of his vehicle and accompanied by a burly, thuggish-looking man. "Let me park this crate. I've got someone here to meet you."

Joe aimed for a nearby vacant spot. He and his friend got out and headed toward Marie. Joe pointed to his friend. "This is the help I came to find – Johnny Klepp – best cop in New Jersey. Johnny this is my niece, Marie. She and Brooke, the friend of the girl I told you about have been tailing that lead from Ocean City." Joe looked worried and asked Marie, "Hey – where's Brooke?"

"I told her to wait in the car. Hang on ..." Marie looked and then grabbed her phone. "She texted me...had to take a bathroom break...in the pizza place down the street. I'll get her back." Marie wiggled her thumbs, quickly put her phone away, and to greet Klepp, simply said, "Hello, John."

Klepp assumed his politest demeanor and said, "Hello,

Marie. I am really pleased to meet anyone related to Jersey Shore Joe." He pointed at Vale's car. "Mind if I ask why you are eye-balling this particular car?"

"The guy driving it almost ran me over. I was about to call Uncle Joe about the woman from the consignment shop. She's inside meeting with the scummiest fat guy I have ever seen. And, before I could get to my car this idiot pulls in without looking and almost flattens me. Then he sprints into the restaurant –"

"And I'll bet he's in there meeting up with your gal and a very large pig of a man named Joey Valentine," interrupted Klepp.

"That's him! How'd you know his name?" asked Marie.

Klepp pointed again to Vale's car. "We were following the guy who almost ran you down. He shot and killed a drug-dealing pimp that worked for Valentine and his partner."

Klepp pointed to the restaurant. "Nick Zebo has a great spot here. Cops, crooks, politicians, good guys, bad guys, tourists with cash – they all come here. Best place in town for a private public meeting. That fat bastard Joey and his partner eat here all the time. So, based on what I know, I guessed. By the way – how'd you know I was talking about *your* fat guy?"

"I bribed the bartender to get his name."

"Good move. You'd make a good detective."

"All I did was toss him a twenty."

"Cops do it all the time. Snitch money solves more cases than anyone wants to admit."

Joe butted in, "Tell me – if Vale shot one of the fat guy's men – why would he come here to meet up with him?"

"He's actually working for the bad guys, too," Kelpp said.

"You seem sure – and not very surprised," Joe

observed.

"Been suspicious since I first laid eyes on him. This figures in with all I know. Vale coming here makes sense – they could meet in the open and nobody would notice. Makes perfect sense. I bet your gal and my guy are bugs in the same web."

"And Joey Valentine is some kinda spider?" asked Marie.

"Maybe, maybe not," Klepp said. "Maybe Joey's just another bug. It's too early to tell. What I do know is that a fat turd named "Lover Boy" Joey Valentine is bad news – and he's obviously involved deeper than just having a drink with my guy. I'd bet my pension on it. Things are starting to come together – your lost girl – the rumored dope – and my dopey partner."

Marie gave him a strained look. "Care to fill me in? You lost me – what partner?"

Klepp pointed and said, "Perry Vale, *the guy in that car,* he's the one we've been tailing – we thought he would lead us to Glenda."

"Glenda?" asked Marie. "Who is Glenda?"

"Big broad – with bigger tits." He looked to Marie and apologized. "Oops, I'm sorry. Anyway – she's the key."

"Now you definitely have me lost!" Marie said.

Klepp smiled, pulled out a cigar, lit it, and explained, "Valentine is your big slob. He runs girls and dope with Tony Carapelli. Both of them are throwbacks to the style of crook that is long past gone – even in Atlantic City. Somehow they got my partner planted in the police with a clean name and background. How? I don't know exactly. But I'll figure it out eventually. The basic information was in the personnel records. They weren't very clever – changed the kid's name from Valentine to Vale – maybe they were just sticking it in our faces. Anyway – Vale was always close – too close – to the Phony Rasta Man. Him you know about – right?"

"Yes – that I do know."

Klepp shook his head. "Boy, I should have seen it! Vale was an inside set of eyes. He served as an alert system to anything we cops had planned. Makes sense – right?"

"Everything except, *Glenda*. Who is she?"

"Okay. She is, or was, one of the phony Jamaican's working girls. She is always with him as his top girl and driver. When your Uncle Joe came asking for help it just happened that his lead to your lost girl and my Glenda are one and the same. So, here we are."

"And where exactly is that?" asked Joe.

"Outside this restaurant waiting for one of them to make a dumb move," answered Klepp with a smirk.

"You sound certain they will," Joe said.

"Their idiot decisions got us this far," Klepp said.

"It's quite a confusing mess," observed Marie. "Who would have thought –"

"Yeah – who would have imagined that independently you could trace the lost girl to Valentine – while Joe ties her to Glenda – who is also tied to Valentine through the Rasta Man. Trust me – everything is linked through Glenda."

"Glenda is a popular girl," remarked Joe.

"Sure is – she has my partner spooked. I'm betting that Vale has realized Glenda knows his phony bust and shootout was just that – a fake – pure and simple. It was put on to cover an execution. He can't use police resources to find her – because if he does – she's going to be under wraps tighter than tight. He's here to get help from his handlers. I'd swear on it. If he finds her before we do, she's dead as dead can be."

"Do you think Glenda is still around?" asked Joe.

"Yes – if she isn't on a bus to California or Timbuktu. My gut sez she's hiding close by."

"Why stay if she saw her friend killed by a cop?" asked Joe.

"Probably needs money – and needs some drugs. She's probably crazy enough to think she can find some." He slapped his head and exclaimed, "Hey – that's it!"

"What is?" asked Joe

"Glenda was constantly with the Rasta Man – almost his shadow. She must know where a pile of cash or a lot of dope is hidden – maybe both."

"So she is still around – waiting for a chance to grab and run?" asked Joe.

"It's either that or she is already long gone and a faint dream."

"If she is gone do you think we'll get any closer to finding out what happened to Jessica by leaning on your ex-partner Valentine and his bosses?" asked Marie.

"Maybe – but I wouldn't count on it. Joey and his type may look comical to us, but they are hard as nails when it comes to talking. I'd bet on Glenda – she's the best way to find out about your lost girl."

"So what do you suggest?" asked Joe.

"We stick to my plan and rely on one of two things. First – we allow my cheesy little ex-partner enough room to do the finding. When he does locate Glenda – we move in – hopefully soon. Or, second, we get a break."

"A break?" asked Joe.

"Yeah – AC is full of snitches." He pointed to Marie. "You already proved that. Maybe some snitch will give Glenda up."

"What's the odds of that happening?" asked Joe.

"If she's around – pretty good. The criminal element – the hustlers, junkies, pimps, pushers, and cheap thieves – they all know one another. Subcultures are all the same, people are people. It ain't rocket science. All the creeps know each other."

"Just like musicians," Joe said.

"Yeah, all communities are similar. I guess –" Klepp halted in mid-sentence. A thought darted from a crevice in his mind.

"You okay?" asked Joe.

"Yeah – yeah – I'm fine," answered Klepp. "It's nothing – just one of those 'senior moments' you hear about. But this time it popped up and stayed."

"Anything useful?" asked Joe.

"Someone is missing."

"That's what I told you. The girl I'm looking for –"

"No. I mean someone else is in the middle of this mess as a link."

"Who?"

"I don't know."

PRETTY BAUBLES

Inside the restaurant Lil sipped her second drink and acted as if time were of no consequence. She knew how to act around Joey and his friends.

Lil, keep your mouth shut, she told herself. *Eventually they will stop posing and ranting, and get around to why I am here. Play it cool, girl – play it cool!*

Finally, Just Tony spoke. "Lemme see those items," he ordered.

Lil reached into her purse as told and extracted the Mermaid jewelry. She discreetly pushed them toward Tony.

He inspected and said, "This stuff is too valuable to waste. I'll take 'em from here. I should have found the right home for them right out." He slipped them into his pocket and motioned for Lil to leave. "Make yourself scarce. I don't want you around – reminds me how you screwed this up."

Lil gathered her purse and while rising said, "I'm sorry – I –"

"Shut up!"

"I – I – just ..."

"I told you to leave. If you weren't Joey's family you'd be in deeper shit than me just being pissed at you. Now go – before I kick your worthless ass all over this joint!"

Lil looked to Joey for support. She got none.

Joey shot her his best 'You Are One Sorry Fuck-up' stare. As the terrified woman departed, he said, "Beat it, Lil. That's the last piece of stuff you'll see from us."

Lil struggled to maintain a shred of composure and pretended to calmly walk away. As she made her way to the exit she came within feet of Perry Vale who looked straight through her. Neither son nor mother displayed a sign of recognition. To any observer, they were strangers.

Once outside, at the edge of the parking lot, Lil bent over the perimeter hedge and retched out everything she had eaten in days.

Damn it, Lil! she screamed within. *They don't fool around – you could be dead over something like this! And, My God! Perry! What do they have on my boy!?*

From across the lot, Johnny Klepp, Joe, and Marie observed Lil. They did not notice Brooke watching them. Brooke edged back into the shadows and texted Marie that she needed more time for her potty break.

Marie felt her phone buzz, looked at the message, and then glanced at her car. She confirmed that Brooke was not back. Joe and Johnny Klepp were focused on Lil and paid no attention to Marie's actions. As they watched Lil pull herself together, Marie said, "Looks like things aren't going her way."

"She's really been shook up," commented Johnny. "More than just put in her place. I say she'll probably head back to Ocean City – to lick her wounds." He nodded toward Marie, "She's still yours to follow."

"Okay. But I've got to find Brooke first."

"She's not back?" asked Joe.

"No."

"Well, you can't leave her in AC."

Í know that. Don't worry I'll find her. What will you two be doing?"

Klepp answered. He pointed to Vale's car and said, "Joe is going to keep watch while I go inside to eyeball the local inhabitants. Your gal got spooked – looks like something very disturbing went down. I'm gonna find out what it was. And maybe I can stir things up even more. Just do your best to keep up with Little Miss Puker."

As the big detective headed into the restaurant Brooke

eased out of the shadows and texted Marie.

"That's Brooke," Marie told Joe as her device vibrated. "We're good to go."

Lil made it to her car and prepared to leave.

"That's your cue," remarked Joe. "Don't lose her."

PLANS

The phone rang once and Erskine Detwilder answered without identifying himself.

"Yes?" he said.

"Mr. D...D...Detwilder?"

"Proceed." His tone had the unmistakable air of coming from one who expected immediate and total obedience.

"I think it's time to c...c...close down the...ah...the...ah...ancillary activities."

"Was I not clear? I've already indicated that."

"I know – I know."

"Then why are you calling me?"

"I had to be c...c...certain."

"Of what?"

"The c...c...costs."

"Which are what?"

"We...ah...we...we...we will need to sa...sa...sacrifice some of our assets in the p...p...police force."

"That's no problem. I told you before – *people do disappear.*"

"I meant...mean...ah...ah all assets...b...b...below me...except maybe one."

"After this call I don't know you. Do as you like."

"I c...c...can use my d...d...discretion?"

"Business models change."

"So it r...r...really is t...t...time?"

"Yes, our investment strategy has matured."

"It's w...w...worked then?"

"Yes, just as planned. Crime and drugs have brought real estate values down as low as they possibly can. With the neighboring states competing with us – cracking the gambling monopoly – it is time to re-create Atlantic City. It will become a more family-friendly destination. We are soon to be Las Vegas East – maybe even Disney North."

"Buy low, s...s...s...sell high never s...s...sounded s...s...so g...good!"

"Simple plans – well thought out – and *executed*." Detwilder gave particular emphasis to this last word.

"So...ah...ah...I..."

"Yes – just as you stated, my friend, you will be the last one standing. If you want to spare someone that's your business, but remember, after today–I do not know you. As I said things change."

There was a long silence.

"Okay...ah...alright. I...ah...ah...just needed to be c...c...certain."

"Fine. As they say, you have to break some eggs to make an omelet. It's time. Break the eggs. "

THE MEN'S ROOM

Klepp loved the men's room at Zebo's. Above the row of urinals, white, pink, and red neon lights whispered, spoke, and then shouted, *Nebo's is the place. Nebo's is the place. Nebo's is the place!*

"Best john in town to piss out expensive liquor – right?" he boomed at the room's sole inhabitant.

From the middle of the porcelain row Perry Vale hosed the wall and nearly wet himself as he spun around to face Klepp.

"Slick move!" taunted the big detective.

"Fuck – Klepp! Don't yell at me!" shouted Vale.

"Shut up, Rookie!"

"Fuck you!"

"Nice attitude But first you better put your dick away. People will talk...then again...they're going to talk *a lot* when it all comes out."

Embarrassed, Vale turned away, zipped, and moved toward the sinks.

"Comes out? What do you mean – comes out? Nothing's coming out – *there's nothing to come out*!" He washed his hands.

"That's not the way I see it."

"Who cares what you see – or think?" He grabbed a paper towel.

"Maybe, Internal Affairs? They care about all kinds of stuff."

"I got through them fine." Vale tossed the towel into the trash bin.

"Sure, Kid, sure. That's why they asked me all about you."

"Me? That's bull." Facing Klepp, Vale said, "I know

you don't like me – you never did."

"I ain't denying it. You do piss me off."

"How? How *exactly* do I piss you off?"

"Cops can lie all they want. They do it all the time. They lie to the suits, the press, their wives – everybody. But they don't lie to their partners."

"Look – I never –"

"Yes you did, Rookie – from day one. You hid stuff – fibbed at first – and then you just plain lied."

"If I did – I had my reasons."

"Like playing for the wrong team?"

"I told you – I'm clean – I passed my interview with IA."

"So you say. But, tell me, Rookie. Why did I get recruited by them?"

"What? That's impossible! You?"

"Yeah – me!"

"So – why are you here?"

"To give notice."

"Notice?"

"Yeah, I know more than you can imagine."

"Like what?"

"A lot."

"You're bluffing."

"No, I'm not bluffing. I'm warning."

"Haw!"

Klepp moved forward and spoke within inches of Vale's face. "When I figure it out. Or better, after I chat it up with Glenda, I'm unloading everything on you with a vengeance." He stepped back and made for the door. On the way he stopped, turned, and said, "For clarification, Rookie. I'm not really pissed at you anymore. If anything I just feel sorry for you. Our side is a mess. It's flawed, screws up, at times it is flat out incompetent, but it tries to do good. You could have found a place, a home, with our side."

Vale stared at the floor.

"Damn, boy, look at me!" Vale did as told. Klepp continued. "Our side even accepts crude alcohol soaked loudmouths like me." Klepp headed to the door. "You can't beat a team like ours, Rookie. My advice is that you find a hole and climb in."

Perry Vale had no comeback. He simply watched Klepp exit the neon-lit room.

VOICES IN MY HEAD

Jeff Breen snapped off the TV and quickly looked around to see if Glenda had seen or heard any of the program's content.

Holy crap! I gotta hide this. I don't want her to know I know anything.

Jeff's other mind, the one that tried to keep him out of trouble, continued to yell at him.

Way to go, idiot! It's got to be her. If it's true – she's hotter than hot. You fool! You knew it was too good to be true – you latching on to a babe wanting to shack up. She wasn't on that road just hitchhiking. She has to be the 'unidentified female accomplice' tied up to the kidnapping. Holy crap! You are on probation. If you get caught up in any of this, it's back to jail!

Jeff hid the remote and tiptoed toward the bedroom door and peeked in to see if Glenda had moved.

Good. She's still zonked out – gives me time to think.

His other mind spoke again.

No – you never think! All you are good for is acting dumb. No – acting dumb-as stupid! From here on let me do the thinking. You – just keep your pecker in check and stay out of my way.

Jeff paced back and forth across the living room of his trailer while his other mind worked at what should be the next move.

You certainly can't tell your Probation Officer about this. POs play it by the letter of the law. Any word about you drinking and doping with a kidnapper and you'll be behind bars again. Best thing to do is to work out a deal with that guy who busted you. He was straight up with you. He seemed sincere when he said he'd help if he could.

He got you a reduced sentence. Yeah – Detective Klepp can be trusted. Well, as much as any cop can be. If he only knew all the stuff she's been telling me about his partner. But, he doesn't and that's my chance for a future. I'm gonna do this – I'm gonna do the right thing!

Jeff stepped outside to make his call.

Klepp, walking out the exit of Nebo's, answered on the third ring. "This better be good," taunted Klepp.

"Detective Klepp?"

"You called – so you know who this is – talk to me."

"I just wanted to be certain."

"Return the favor – who's this?

"Jeff – Jeff Breen."

There was a pause. "Pot bust – a couple a years ago. Your first – right?"

"Yeah – yeah. That was me."

"So?"

"So – ah – well..."

"I'm not on your Christmas card list – so, you must want something. What is it?"

"Well – sorta – I – I –"

"Come on – come on. I'm into something important and can't waste my time."

"I know something –"

"Then spit it out!"

"I know about the guy who was killed in the Pine Barrens."

"Yeah – so what! Everyone knows about it – been on TV. Jeff, tell me something nobody knows."

"He wasn't alone."

"Go on."

"There was a witness..."

"Keep going."

"The whole thing was seen by a girl."

"Glenda."

154

"How'd you know?"

"I'm clairvoyant."

"What?"

"I'm a good guesser."

"Uh..."

"And, I guess she's strung out and scared – very scared."

"Wow! You are – cla –"

"Clairvoyant! It comes with my others gifts. Now cut the crap – tell me what else you know."

"I – I – I know where she'll be in about an hour."

"You guessing or do you really know?"

"I – I really know. I'm her wheels to pick up some stuff before she blows town for the north part of the shore."

Klepp laughed. "And you called me because you are such a solid citizen, right?"

"It's something like that."

"Tell me what the 'something like that' means."

"I've got some things hanging over me..."

"Serious stuff?"

"Nothing big – but just enough to screw me with my PO."

"Still smoking?"

"Yeah...I had...I had a bad piss test. I'm sure to lose my job – it's a good one – on the road crew."

"I might be able to help with the test."

"Good – good – that's good. I want – I need to start over."

"That's nice. So – tell me, Jeff. Where does Glenda and her big tits show up in an hour?"

Jeff snickered.

"It ain't funny!"

"Sure – sure! On South Carolina. You know the motel a block from the beach?"

"I know it."

"The place she's going to is two doors closer to the water. I'm taking her there – in my blue pickup. Look for my blue truck."

"I'll be there. You deliver her and then sit tight."

"You mean I can't leave – I have to stay?"

"Exactly. She's expecting you to be her ride in and out. If she gets spooked she's coming straight back to your truck. That requires you being there."

"Oh – I see." His voice went faint and wispy.

"Don't flake on me, Jeff. If you want a clean start – a fresh record – you have to do this."

"Okay, okay – I'm good – I'll do it."

"Fine. Now, forget you called me and act natural. Don't spook Glenda!"

Klepp ended the call and punched in a new number. When the ring was answered he said, "Listen, I need some back up. If you want to coast until retirement – get your ass to the motel on South Carolina – the one a block from the beach. You can help me collar Glenda – the girl running from the LBI kidnapping." He did not wait for a reaction or reply. "You need this – and I know why." He ended the call and quickly made a second one to the Reliable Cab Company. In seconds he barked, "Lou, this is Johnny. Send your quickest guy to Zebo's. I need a lift – like ten minutes ago!" After getting confirmation Klepp told a puzzled Joe what was up. "I've got a hot lead on Glenda. It may be bogus, but my gut sez to pounce on it."

"I can drive. Why call a cab?" Joe asked.

"We can't lose Vale. You dog him. If my lead is bad one of Lou's boys will get me get back to you. Give me your cell number." In the time they exchanged numbers one of Lou's cabs appeared. Klepp repeated his instructions, "Just stay with Vale"

Joe was left in the parking lot with his thoughts.

Johnny might be right. Maybe everything is

connected – music and crime have something in common: people. The trick is to figure out how it's all linked together.*

He hummed a tune, leaned against his car, and continued to watch for Vale.

Not long ago all I thought of was sanding an old boat and schlepping around as a hotel handyman. Now I'm knee deep in...what?

~ ~ ~

Inside the restaurant Tony Caparelli looked at the incoming call's number, grinned, and motioned for his companions to tone it down. There was immediate silence.

"Yeah – talk to me," he said and then listened. "Uh huh – yeah – sure, I suppose I would like that to happen." Although the others at the table acted as if they could not hear Tony's side of the conversation they all silently strained to pick up some shred of information. "If this goes the way you say it should...I think I can arrange something special for you," he told the caller. He listened to the response and ended the call with, "Go ahead – Just don't screw it up." Everyone at the table pretended not to hear the remark. Conversation resumed, and after a few moments Tony signaled for Joey to follow him away from the table.

In a quiet corner of the restaurant Tony leaned toward Joey and whispered instructions. Tony returned to the table and Joey made his way to the bar to order more drinks. At the bar Perry Vale got up to leave, but Joey blocked his departure.

Joey leaned toward Vale and words were exchanged.

A visibly agitated Vale protested. Joey leaned closer, whispered, and Vale deflated like a popped balloon. A second whisper got him moving. Vale got out of the establishment as fast as any man could.

BETRAYAL

Glenda pointed to an open spot down the street from the motel.

"Park there," she told Jeff. "Wait for me no matter how long it takes. Can you do that?"

He's my back-up ride out of here and nothing more. I'm getting what I need then I am gone!

"Sure – sure," Jeff replied without much enthusiasm. *I hope this is over fast.*

"I mean it," she ordered. *He's acting really strange.*

"I said 'okay!'" *Damn, I want this to be over.*

"What's with you? You've been acting funny." *Creepy is more like it.*

"It's nothing." *I hope Klepp is here.*

"Nothing? Better be." *After I get the stuff I'm gonna dump this idiot-loser.*

Glenda sensed that Jeff was uptight. To calm him and keep him off-guard she said, "Just relax – this won't take long. I'll be in and out before you know it." *Yeah, I'll just head down the boardwalk and leave him sitting here waiting.*

Glenda slipped into a dark blue hooded sweatshirt, donned a baseball cap, and slinked out of the truck. She plunged her hands into the hoodie's pockets and shuffled past the motel looking in no way like the songstress she wanted to be nor the street-hustler that she had actually become.

Jeff adjusted the truck's mirrors, slid down into his seat, and watched. As he was telling himself that Klepp was too late, he saw a figure step out of the shadows and follow Glenda. *Thank God Klepp's here! Now, all I have to do is wait, let him cuff her, and then I can go home.*

From his position Jeff could not see South Ocean a block away. It was there that Perry Vale parked his car and cautiously made his way to the buildings on South Carolina from the rear.

Neither Jeff nor Vale saw Joe arrive and park in the alleyway behind the buildings. From his unseen location Joe thought, *I must admit that I'm confused. I understand why I'm following Johnny's partner. Maybe he'll lead me to Glenda, who can lead me to where Jessie is, or at least give me information of what happened to her. What I don't understand is "why me?"*

Joe got out of his car and walked slowly along the route that he had seen Vale take. *I'm not trained in this cloak and dagger stuff. I guess I should see where he goes and then double back to watch his car. I hope I don't lose him.*

Joe was a dozen steps away from his car when he heard the shots. *Boom! Boom!* There was a pause. Then came *Bang! Bang!* Another pause, followed by *Boom! Boom!* again.

What on earth! Joe thought. He looked about for other people, saw none, and decided to investigate alone. *You're nuts to do this by yourself,* he thought as he approached the back entrance to the building that he assumed Vale had entered. At the rear door he heard a commotion. Someone was clumsily descending the staircase and before he could react the door swung open.

"Jesus!" cried Joe when he saw a blood drenched Johnny Klepp.

"Joe?" rasped Klepp as he fell forward. Joe grabbed Klepp, easing him to the ground as the injured man wheezed, rasped, and whispered, "Tell the coffee man I didn't see it coming...I never thought... my partner would...would..." He did not finish.

"Hold on, man, hold on!" shouted Joe. Klepp did not

answer. A soft gurgling sound came from his chest. "Jesus, Johnny! You can't die! No! Oh, Jesus! You just can't, man, no!"

Joe checked the big man's pulse and found none. He pressed and blew as taught, but there was no response. He kept trying. There was no effect. He tried again, and still there was nothing. Finally, Joe stopped, and fumbled for his cell phone. Blood smattered fingers pressed nine-one-one.

The operator spoke, "9-1-1 what is your emergency?"

"My friend...is...is... He is dead. He's a police officer."

From that point on so much happened that Joe remembered very little.

BLUE LIGHT SPECIAL

From the edge of a sea of blue and red lights Jeff Breen watched the police maneuver in and out of the building and its grounds. Four ambulances and a fleet of patrol units filled the space between him and where the shootings occurred. A double band of yellow crime scene tape circled the area creating an island of police procedure.

"I'm fucked," Jeff murmured. "I'm totally fucked." *Klepp must think I set him up. If I leave – he'll believe it for sure. If I stay – maybe I have a chance at convincing him that I knew nothing about what went down – whatever it is. Shit! I can't see anything from here. Where's Klepp? I gotta find out what happened. Think, dude, think!*

An idea came to him and Jeff quickly returned to his truck, rummaged through the cab, donned his orange iridescent safety vest with the yellow stripes, grabbed a flashlight and then an emergency tool box. *This might fool 'em.* He told himself. *I need to get past that yellow tape.*

It was easier than he imagined. Jeff walked up to the tape, lifted it up, slid under, and continued walking. No one objected to what seemed to be one of their own taking a short cut. Inside the taped off area Jeff moved casually toward the nearest ambulance and attempted to blend in. He was so focused on getting to the vehicle that he did not see the approaching gurney.

"Stand back, or lend us a hand," a butch EMT ordered.

Jeff jumped sideways. "Sorry – I –"

Before he could finish his apology, she barked, "Grab hold! This is a heavy one." Jeff did as told and assisted the EMT and her partner in placing the loaded gurney into the vehicle. "Thanks, man," she said.

"Sure – no problem," mumbled Jeff.

To her partner, Jeff, and to no one in particular, she said, "I never thought I'd load Johnny Klepp into my wagon."

"Klepp?" blurted Jeff. "Detective Klepp?"

"Yeah – Big Boy himself. Took it in the chest – at close range."

Jeff froze.

The EMT rattled on. "He made quite a mess. Bled out running down the back stairs. Hell of a shootout. Klepp's partner and the shooter bought it, too. Three dead on four shots. We thought there was a fourth casualty, but was only three. Damnedest thing – blood was all over him. Guess who it was?" Jeff was still frozen. The EMT ignored his silence and continued. "Jersey Shore Joe – *that's who!* Imagine that! I listened to him on the radio for years. What the hell he was doing in the middle of this isn't clear. But he was first on the scene – got covered in blood head to toe trying to resuscitate Klepp." She nodded toward the gurney. "Didn't do him any good – Klepp was a goner."

At the mention of Joe's name Jeff awoke from his trance. "Are you certain it was Jersey Shore Joe?"

"Yeah – none other. He attempted to help – gave it a hell of a try." She pointed. "He's over there – pretty shook up."

Jeff's eyes followed her point and he spotted Joe seated between two plainclothes cops. *That's him alright. Jeez – it looks like he's been through hell.*

The EMT's partner slammed the ambulance's doors shut and declared, "Time to roll."

Jeff grabbed his gear, waved goodbye, and headed toward Joe. *If I hang around maybe I'll hear more about what went down.* When he got within earshot of where Joe sat he dropped his toolbox and used it as a stool. *Stay cool – act like you belong.*

Plain Clothes Cop Number One said to Joe, "Mr. Kontos, we can have someone drive you home.

"No, I'm fine – really."

"At least let us find you a new shirt," Cop Number Two offered.

Joe looked down his front and nodded. "Yes – yes – I would appreciate that."

Cop Number One disappeared while Cop Number Two stayed put. "We've got your statement, but since this incident involves three deaths and two of them police officers, we'd appreciate your keeping us informed of your whereabouts." Joe looked up.

"You don't suspect –"

"No – no," the cop interrupted, "it's nothing like that." He paused, sighed heavily, and continued. "This is such a damned mess! That's the long and short of it. The press will have a field day – two dead cops – a civilian dead – and..."

Cop Number One returned, said, "Here's a new shirt," and handed it to Joe.

"Thanks." Joe stood up, put it on, and looked about. "Is it okay for me to go now?"

Cop Number Two answered, "Yes – no problem." He reached into his pocket and pulled out a business card. "Here," he said, "If you think of anything, and I mean *anything*, just give me a call."

Joe took the card and mechanically placed it in his wallet. "Sure," he said, "if I recall anything else – I'll call." He shook both cops' hands and left.

As Joe disappeared Cop Number Two said, "Based on what he told us and the mess upstairs, I'd say it's a gun happy rookie and his burnt out partner screwing things up. Klepp pushed Vale's buttons at Zebo's and they crossed paths again too soon. Bad judgment all around –

lead flies, much too quickly, and we have what we have – a public relations nightmare. Vale was on admin leave because of the other shooting, and Klepp was working for us."

"So tell me, Rich," how did the girl get in the middle of it?"

"Stupidity – dumb luck – bad karma? She was the Rasta Man's number one. Klepp and Vale must have been looking for her. Maybe they were tailing her. What we know works if she was followed by Klepp and she shoots at Vale, who was waiting for her. Then Vale bangs her *and Klepp* thinking that Klepp was her back up or accomplice. The girl's small caliber weapon hit the mark, but gave Vale enough time to fire back – that's how he had time to get the girl and Klepp – with one shot each. Then he succumbs to his wounds."

"Makes sense. If Klepp is behind the girl – then he stumbles down the stairs –"

"– and into Jersey Shoe Joe Kontos' arms –"

"– yeah – and dies."

"Jesus – what a friggin' mess!"

"Tell me about it – and we have zip to show for it."

"Not a thing. With Vale and Klepp dead we don't have much."

"Kontos' tale about his search for the missing girl is interesting, but it has no connection to us in Internal Affairs that I can see."

"His lost girl could have been one of the Jamaican's."

"Could explain Klepp chasing down the big blonde."

"It looks as if Klepp was doing double duty – helping a friend and tailing Vale for us. Kontos was tagging along behind Vale as told and then paths crossed – and bullets flew."

"Makes sense."

"Kontos was legitimately first on the scene – if you

believe what little he told us."

"I do."

"Too bad he's a wreck – doesn't recall anything beyond hearing two booms, two bangs, and then another two booms. Six shots – when we've only got four gunshot wounds and no errant hits anywhere within the crime scene."

"I've seen the stupor he's in before. It looks like a classic case of Transient Global Amnesia – trauma caused, instant onset, and specific in the time period it covers. It leaves the victim with personality, awareness, and a set of symptoms like his – headache, nausea, cold hands and feet, vomiting, and trembling."

"So, do we cut him lose?"

"Do we have a choice? In essence we already have."

"Yeah, you're right – he doesn't know anything that can help us. The kid that called in the tip and Klepp's call to that throwaway cell is the only thing we have."

"The kid's a low level loser. I bet if we locate him he knows nothing more than what he told Klepp on the call."

"Put a BOLO on the kid anyway."

"Will do."

"Then...we focus on that final call by Klepp. It's our trail."

"And it's near to impossible to trace – that's why *they* use 'em."

"Yeah – and we don't have a clue who *they* are."

"You don't honestly think Klepp was dirty – do you?"

"I don't know – I just don't know. What he said on the call may have been payback for an old debt."

"Could we have misjudged him?"

"I hope we didn't."

"Me, too. Let's call it a night and start over tomorrow.

"Doing what?"

"Examining every person in his past – maybe we'll

167

catch a break."

"Like finding the kid?"

"Yeah, it'd be a start."

Everything the two plainclothes cops had said was clearly heard by Jeff who was still perched on his toolbox.

They mentioned me! Jeff screamed inside. *They know who I am! And I thought I had a problem with my P.O. before. I'm cooked. What does Jersey Shore Joe have to do with all this – and does he know anything about me and Klepp? I need to ease out of here, crank up my truck, and quietly disappear. My piss test is nothing compared to this – I'll deal with it later, if I'm not in jail!*

SHE'S GONE

Joe woke up late the next morning and for a brief time believed the previous night's events were a dream. That was until he saw the mess in the bathroom. If the red smears on the sink and blood stained towel could not remind him of what had actually happened, then the Boom Boom! Bang Bang! Boom Boom! sound track playing in his head would.

It was real, he told himself. *I've never been that close to death before. What's happening? What am I involved in? One girl's disappearance has proven to be part of so much more – and the deaths of Johnny, his partner, and Glenda have created one huge dead end. I need to talk to Marie. After last night the woman in the consignment store is all we've got.*

Joe dressed, looked for his niece, and found her making coffee in the B and B's kitchen.

"You look as bad as I feel," Marie told him.

"When I tell you what happened last night – you'll feel worse."

Over coffee Joe shared his account of the previous night's events.

"Oh my God, it's terrible," bemoaned Marie. "Three people dead and we are no closer to finding what happened to Brooke's friend, Jessie. Now we have nowhere else to go."

"We still have the woman in the shop to lean on."

"No we don't."

"What do you mean?"

"She's gone." Marie got glum. "It's my turn to talk about a terrible night – and why I feel so rotten."

"Go easy. Take your time."

"I got in late, Uncle Joe, very late. You were already asleep when I returned. If I had any idea what happened."

"It wouldn't have helped. I think I passed out."

"Still – I wish I'd known what you had gone through."

"I'm fine now. Tell me what happened after you left the restaurant."

"We followed her – just like before. Brooke was a great extra set of eyes."

"Tell me what happened."

"The woman – Lil – she came straight back to the shop, thrashed around inside for a while, and came out with two suitcases. Whatever happened at the restaurant really set her off – she looked a sight. She acted scared. No – terrified – she was terrified. Into the car went the suitcases and – zoom! She moved fast and drove even faster. It was tough to follow her, but we did."

"Where to?"

"That's the bad news."

"Go on."

"She just kept driving and driving, but going nowhere. She looped and circled a lot. We were about to run out of gas, I had to pull over, and we lost her. Uncle Joe, I'm sorry." Marie looked devastated.

"It can't be helped, Marie. We're not pros. Neither you nor I are cut out for this."

"How do we handle Brooke? What do we tell her?"

"The truth, that we tried our best. She knows that. Brooke is smart – way beyond her years. She can handle it – I'm sure."

"So it's over?"

Joe sighed. "There's not much left to go on."

"But we just can't quit."

"I guess I could nose around the consignment shop one last time. Maybe I'll get lucky and find something. I'll give it one last peek."

"Really?'

"Yes – but only after I take a long walk. Last night pushed me off my foundation. I need to think." He got up and gave Marie a fatherly hug. "I need some boardwalk time."

"Sure – sure, Uncle Joe," answered a concerned Marie.

Joe placed his cup by the sink, left by the rear door, and headed for the beach with the gunshot soundtrack still playing in his ears. He was in his own world and did not notice that Brooke was standing within earshot. He also did not notice the blue truck parked across the street as he left the inn and headed for the boardwalk.

BANG! BANG! BANG!

"Just Tony" Carapelli often proclaimed that his success was built upon an uncanny ability to foresee the moves made by the people around him. He was particularly boastful about an ability to anticipate the moves of those who feared him. Tony was full of himself and very mistaken. In the end, he never saw the end coming.

Joey Valentine was stinking up the building again and could not respond when the doorbell rang. From inside the fouled john, he shouted, "Tony, you better get that!"

Eager to get some fresh air, Tony yelled back, "Don't move. I'm on it!" He opened the door, recognized the caller, frowned, and said with scorn, "What the fuck are you doin' here?"

There was no answer. Tony turned to lead the visitor inside. He heard a faint "whoosing," and a silenced bullet ping ponged inside his skull. He was dead before he hit the floor. So much for Tony's skill at anticipating the moves of others.

From his porcelain perch Joey shouted, "Hey, Tony! Who was that?"

No answer.

From inside the john Joey called out his apology, "Damn it, Tony, I'm sorry! You know how it is when I gotta go." He broke into laughter. "Boy, oh, Boy!"

In a few minutes Joey finished laughing, flushed, and opened the door. What he viewed was the last thing he could have imagined.

"What the hell!" Joey blurted out when he saw his partner stretched out in a pool of blood. The air carried another soft whoosh and a second bullet found its target.

Joey's head exploded and he collapsed like a bag of

173

fertilizer dropped from the roof.

For several minutes the shooter stood silent near both bodies.

Lil DeNova finally said, "You were always nothing more than a stinking pig, Joey. I put up with you and this piece of shit partner of yours for years. I did your bidding – never complained. But you couldn't leave my boy alone. You just had to ruin him. He's dead. My boy is dead. Because of you I have nothing."

The distraught woman took a deep breath, placed the weapon in her mouth, and pulled the trigger.

WHO'S HE?

On his fifth time of walking past Mia's Christmas Gallery Joe realized that he had lost track of time.

The boardwalk does that, he thought. *It magically soothes the soul by altering time. I've been on the boards for hours, but it seems like I've been walking just a few minutes. Time moves slower the closer you are to the water. Maybe I should check out the consignment shop again.*

Joe left the boardwalk and headed to the consignment shop on Asbury. Boom Boom! Bang Bang! Boom Boom! played in his head. Again, he did not notice the blue truck, nor the young man watching him walk the half-mile to the shop.

When Joe arrived at the shop he found an Ocean City Police cruiser parked in front and two officers at the door.

"Mind if I ask 'what's going on?'" he asked.

"You work here?" countered the older officer.

Joe told the truth and then fibbed. "No. But I was coming here to meet with the owner."

"Did you know the owner, Lil DeNova?" the officer asked in his most official tone.

Joe picked up on the use of the past tense. "Yes, I guess you could say I *know* her – what happened?"

Without thinking the junior officer blurted, "She's dead – involved in a shooting. We're here to secure the place until Atlantic City PD gets –"

"That's enough," interrupted the older one. He read Joe's concern and probed, "What exactly is your reason for being here? How well did you know her?"

Joe fended off the authoritarian move with, "I only knew her through the business. I'm here *only* for that."

The cop countered with, "Can I see some ID? Mister – ah –"

"Kontos – Joseph Kontos. And, 'no' I do not have my ID on me. Is that a problem?" he snapped back.

The cop finally recognized Joe's voice and grinned. "Joe Kontos? As in Jersey Shore Joe Kontos?"

Joe relaxed and allowed a small smile to smear his face. "Yes – I've been called that."

"Damn! I'm sorry, Joe," the cop apologized. He stuck his hand out, grabbed Joe's, and pumped. "Really sorry, man!"

The junior cop looked confused and asked, "You know him, Ed?"

"Know him? Damn! In my day we worshipped him."

Joe blushed some. Ed went on. "Joe here was 'The Man! In the late 60s and 70s the shore wasn't the shore without him. Jersey Shore Joe was everywhere – singing, spinning records, DJ-ing parties, hosting events, opening shopping centers – he did everything. You name it he did it!"

"You're too kind," offered Joe. "And, you're exaggerating."

"No way – absolutely no way!"

Joe allowed his blush to fade and used the goodwill as a platform to learn more about Lil DeNova's demise. "Ed, could you share with me some more about what happened?"

Ed was thrilled to be on a first name basis with a local legend and replied without pause, "Sure – sure, Joe." He waved off his partner and stepped closer. "Get this. Local mild mannered shopkeeper, Lil DeNova, sauntered into a known mob joint and nailed two of Atlantic City's nastiest hoods *with one shot each!*"

"Really?" Joe played the wowed innocent.

"Really! Then she swallowed the gun barrel and,

Boom! She off'd herself on the spot."

"What would cause her to do that?" asked Joe.

"Who in creation knows?" Ed pointed at the shop. "We've been asked to sit on this place until the AC boys get here. Nobody in or out – that's what we were told."

The finality of the situation hit Joe, and he said, "I guess that ends it for me."

"Yeah – I'm sorry," chimed Ed, "but you aren't going to be doing any business here. I've seen places locked tighter than tight over stuff like this. I bet the feds will be in on it – those guys she wasted being 'connected' and all. She must have been into something really bad to end it like that."

Joe wanted to leave.

I've got to tell Marie and Brooke about this. We've definitely hit what looks to be the final dead end.

Joe pressed his new best friend. "Ed, if anything peculiar turns up would you be willing to let me know?"

"Peculiar? In what way?"

"A missing person."

"Missing person? I thought you had business here?"

"Yes I did. I have reason to believe that Jessie Collier's jewelry was here and – ."

"I know that name," the younger cop said quickly. Both men looked to him. "Wild kid – I took the report on her – nothing to it. She's a typical runaway."

Brooke's original wall thought Joe. *I understand what she was up against.*

"In any event – if there's any mention of her – will you let me know?"

"Sure, Joe," answered Ed, "you can count on it."

"Thanks, I guess I'll head home," Joe said as he shook Ed's hand and waved goodbye to the unimpressed younger cop.

As Joe walked away Ed remarked to his companion,

"Imagine that – in his day he was *really* somebody. Now look at him. He's just another retiree shuffling around looking for something to do."

"Yeah, and wasting his time."

Joe walked. If he could have heard the comments made about his decline he might have cared. But his mind was occupied. The Boom Boom! Bang Bang! Boom Boom! beat played on and on in his head.

Again, he walked past the parked truck without noticing it or its driver.

WHO SHOT JOHN?

Malone poked his head into the Internal Affairs workroom and asked, "Want me to ruin your day?"

Rich Kona looked up from reading a folder and said, "Sure, give it a try. But I guarantee you can't. Not after I tell you about this." He pointed down at his reading material.

Malone craned his neck to peek. "Is that the ballistics report on Klepp and Vale?"

"Yep."

"Bad?"

"Bad would be good. Sit down and I will ruin your day – all of it."

Malone pulled a chair to the closest spot and said, "Fire away."

Kona summarized the report. "We've got four bullet wounds in three bodies. Some amazing shots, very accurate, and, obviously, quite deadly. But, in and of themselves, they are no problem."

"So what is?"

"Two of the bullets – the kill shots on Klepp and the girl – do not match Vale's weapon."

"That means?"

"– we definitely have another gun – which is missing. And we possibly have another shooter who is unknown."

"Ugh!"

"Right! But there's more – we probably have a set up crime scene. "

"How so?"

"The GSR on both Vale's shooting hand and the girl's are smudged and unevenly distributed. To me that means we've got a staged event. Somebody placed the GSR on

179

them."

"Shit!"

"Oh I'm sorry. Did I ruin your day?"

"Smart ass – you ruined a week. Maybe the whole month."

EMANCIPATED

Marie was perplexed. She had spoken to Brooke about why her parents failed to return from their travels to handle the repercussions of her "escape" from boarding school and Brooke seemed remarkably unconcerned.

"Messages go out and none return," Brooke said with amazing calm. "It doesn't surprise me. They haven't shown interest in my life in a long time. Don't worry about me. I'm cool with it"

All attempts to reach the Paxtons had failed. So, by default, the decision was made that Brooke would remain in Ocean City. Marie and Joe would serve informally as her guardians and she would earn her keep by working at the inn.

"I'm a slave," Brooke joked when the details were agreed upon, "But I'm a willing one."

In addition to working at the inn, Brooke took an unusual interest in assisting Joe with the *Summerwind's* renovations. Joe was glad for the help and, more so, for the company. He used the boat as a retreat to mend from his experience with death and found Brooke to be great company.

"I admit that I'm taken by the girl," he told Marie after several days of him and Brooke working together. "She's like another niece."

"More like a lapdog," quipped Marie.

"Jealous?"

"No – more like cautious."

"Cautious? Why?"

"I see things."

"Like what?"

"Just things. Maybe it's nothing."

"If you see something – it can't be nothing. You need to explain."

"Well…" She hesitated.

"Out with it."

"She plays you…all the time."

"What?!"

"I said, 'Brooke plays you.'"

"Plays me? What do you mean?"

"I mean…like a woman plays a man."

"C'mon, Marie – that's a bit much."

"For a girl her age she has…has…"

"Has what?"

"She has a look of experience that is not *normal.* Nor is it healthy. I see it come out when she's working you."

"Working me?"

"Yes, *like a woman works a man.*"

"I'll be damned. You are jealous!"

"No. I'm worried." Marie stared at her uncle. "You've been in such a funk since your detective friend was killed. You avoid people, except Brooke, and in general, you're not yourself."

"I'm not avoiding anyone. I plan to attend Johnny's funeral. And as to my general state, of well-being, I am processing."

"Processing? I'd say it's more like post-traumatic stress, or something similar."

"Maybe something similar – like *processing*?"

"Call it what you will, but it has made you vulnerable to Brooke's wiles."

"How would you know?"

"I've done a lot watching."

"Snooping?"

"Of course not. Just watching. I felt it was my responsibility."

"Responsibility?"

"I had to do something."

"Really?"

"Yes – really."

"Is this where I listen?"

"It would be good. You've gone through a lot. You can't see it. It could be what your mind does to avoid and compensate. It's a natural self-protective response made by the brain. You went through a terrible shock and your brain is struggling to make sense of it all. Memory loss, decreased attention span – it's PTSD in some form. You are functional, but to be safe I'm keeping an eye on you and Brooke."

"You sound like a shrink."

"No, you said it. I'm just a jealous woman." She stuck out her tongue and grimaced.

"So – I was right!"

"Relax, Uncle Joe. I'm just being cautious and protective."

"Protective – of me? Please – I'm just a broke, burnt-out, over-the-hill, music junkie."

"Not to me. To me you're an expensive gift wrapped in brown paper."

"My – my – my! You have matured beyond your years."

"Don't make light of this, Uncle Joe. And don't get me wrong. I like Brooke, but..."

"But what?"

"I don't know. I just don't know why she likes you so much."

"And you think *my* brain is struggling. Brooke likes me because I'm...likeable. And I am a natural father figure. Remember, we both took interest in her quest to find out what happened to her friend, Jessie. Admit that you like her."

"Okay, I admit that I have nothing to go on beyond my intuition. But just be careful.

"Be careful? Of what?"

"I don't know...I just don't know."

THE SEND-OFF

The prayer ended and music began. Mary Clamson wiped an imaginary tear from her left eye, sniffed, and expelled an audible sigh.

That's all I've got, she thought. *This memorial service is such a sham. Why do they bother to have one at all?*

She looked about the room and took note of how many and who had shown up for the quickly arranged event. A smirk came and went from her face.

The hypocrites! They're just covering their butts. They have to honor a fallen cop – but not too publically – he might have shot his partner on purpose. Jeez! And then there's the other funeral. Vale's the hero who wasted the scum that snuffed the All American kid from LBI – and he may have shot his partner, too!

Mary scanned the crowd.

This is a public relations mess for the ages. Career cops being told to show up out of uniform to honor the fallen heroes – and the fallen heroes may have killed each other.

She scanned the room again and stopped on a familiar face.

Well I'll be – it's Joe Kontos. Haven't seen him in ages – not since the days when I was moonlighting on security details. When this is over I've got to say "hello." I wonder if he'll remember me.

After the service Mary approached Joe and asked "You're Joe Kontos – Jersey Shore Joe – right?" She punctuated her statement with a broad inviting smile.

"Yes, I am," affirmed Joe. His eyes shot downward and fixed on her bosom, as he mumbled. "Do I know you?" His stare was aimed at the line between her breasts and the piece of jewelry resting there.

Uncomfortable with Joe staring at her cleavage Mary quickly answered, "I hope so. I'm Mary – Mary Clamson – one of Johnny's old partners. Do you remember me? As a rookie cop I did a lot of security gigs. Some were for you."

"Sure, sure – I remember. " Joe caught himself and tried to look up away from her chest where the distinctive mermaid necklace rested. All his adult life Joe had been keenly aware of the male's natural propensity to look for feminine folds of skin. He always fought this instinct and acted like a gentleman. But now it took all the restraint Joe had within to divert his gaze and say, "That's an amazing piece of jewelry – tell me about it."

Thank God! Mary thought. *For a second I'd have sworn he had turned into just another old letch.* She answered, "Thank you for noticing. Yes, it is amazing. And actually, it's new. A friend surprised me with it as a gift just a few days ago."

Joe wanted to stare but forced his eyes to look away.

That's Jessie's – I know it!

A wave of nausea hit him and he was tossed behind the building on South Carolina and vividly experienced a traumatic montage in real time. Joe heard shots, clearly saw Klepp's bloody chest, caught him falling, and this time he remembered his friend's final words.

I must remember what Johnny said!

He ordered his mind to work. Joe's head raced.

She's Johnny's partner? Mermaid jewelry! Coffee Man? Boom Boom! Bang Bang! Boom Boom! He said it was his partner!

His head raced even more.

Boom Boom! Bang Bang! Boom Boom!

It was too much. Joe fainted and fell backward, crashing onto the floor.

"Oh my God!" exclaimed Mary.

"Call the medics!" was yelled in unison by a chorus of Johnny's booze-laden colleagues.

The EMTs arrived. Joe was moved to a couch in a private area, unconscious and unaware of the commotion he had caused. Calm soon returned and by the time Joe was over the effects of smelling salts, the hall was emptying, and he was only vaguely aware that two of Johnny Klepp's ex-partners exited together.

As they left, the one said, "I'd swear in c...c...court that t...t...that t...t...that dirty old p...p...perv was looking at your b...b ...boobs and the sight of them s...s...struck him down."

"Bill Coyle, I swear you are *so* male – so lame and so very very male," Mary told him.

"S...s...sorry, b...b...but he was s...s...staring."

"Yes, at my necklace."

"Why?"

"Christ! How should I know?"

"Where d...d...did it c...c...come from?"

"Tony gave it to me."

"S...S...SHIT!"

"I can't believe you are jealous of a dead man."

"It's j...j...just –"

"Relax! The necklace is nothing. Trust me, it's got nothing to do with anything. Forget about it."

"I'll t...t...try."

THE TAIL

It took some talking, but Joe convinced the EMTs that he was able to navigate on his own and reluctantly they set him loose. Outside the funeral home his brain went into overdrive at the sight of the blue truck that had been showing up in his life. Initially he had missed it, but its constant presence finally made him aware that he was being followed. Without thought Joe forced his wobbly legs to head straight for the vehicle parked across the street. The driver saw him coming and slumped down into the seat.

Joe tapped on the window and ordered, "Roll it down!"

Jeff Breen sheepishly complied. His faced revealed that he knew he had been busted.

"We need to talk!" barked Joe. "I know you've been following me!"

"Well – I – I – really –"

"Out with it," yelled Joe, "I'm not in the mood for any bullshit!"

"I – I – I –"stuttered Jeff, "I – I –"

"Listen up! I put two and two together and come up with at least four times that this junker and you have been tailing me. You're either a stalker or some creep tied up in Johnny Klepp's death – which is it?"

"I – I – I – I – " Jeff could not form a second word. His face contorted, he snorted, sobbed, and began to cry like a toddler. "I'm sorry Joe – but you told me that –"

"What!?"

Between sobs, Jeff gasped, "– you t – t – told me a guy could –"

"Wait!" Joe shouted, "*I told you? Me?* What the hell! I

don't know you – never saw you in my life." Joe realized that he was not getting anywhere by pressing. He backed off a bit. Calmly he said, "Okay, just tell me why you are following me."

Jeff held up both hands in a defensive motion, wiped his nose on his sleeve, and said as loud as he could, "I was the last guy to call in on your last show. Remember? I'm Jeff, the guy you t – t – told – ." Jeff took a deep breath and said, "You said, you said, a guy could start over if he tried. You said that on your show."

"Hold on – you're a fan. *Are you stalking me?*"

"No – no, Joe. It's not like that. You said one guy can change things. I'm here because of that...and Klepp."

"*Now I am confused!*" lamented Joe. He pointed to the front of the cab and said, "Clear a spot. I need to sit down."

Jeff nodded exuberantly and made room by pushing a pile of seat junk into the console. "Yeah – yeah – sure!"

Joe got in, leaned back in the seat, and sighed.

"Now let me get this straight – you were the guy who called right before I quit. You're a fan, but not a nut-job. And you are following me because you are involved in what happened to Johnny Klepp – right?"

"Right! I –"

"Wait! My head is pounding!" He leaned forward and held his head in both hands. "Jeez – I feel like my brain is in a Cuisinart."

"I'm sorry, Joe. I really am sorry," Jeff said. His remorse was sincere. His face showed concern for Joe and fear for his own situation. "I'm scared. I was following you because I thought I could trust you."

Joe responded. "Just tell me what happened – in your *simplest* words." He leaned back and closed his eyes. "I'm listening."

Jeff did a good job. He quickly recounted his

involvement in finding and helping Glenda and steering Klepp to her after he had learned that Glenda was a witness to what happened in the Pine Barrens. When Jeff finished, Joe asked, "Is that everything?"

"No, I kept it simple, but there's more."

"Let me hear it all."

"Glenda was a non-stop motor mouth. She was either singing or yacking away, and she'd mix things all together. I knew early on that I made a mistake in giving her a lift. I've done some real dumb stuff when it comes to girls. Right off, I was snowed by her, but then I got concerned. She'd drop stuff in the middle of a statement, or a song. She told me some real scary stuff."

"Like what?"

"Like how she knew about the girls being used and the parties."

"Parties?"

"You know for sex."

"Go on."

"Some were being doped, OD'ing, even being killed."

Joe sat up. "Tell me more."

"She said the dude she was with –"

"The Rasta guy?"

"Yeah him. She told me how he got tight with some girl who lured younger ones into his group. She explained how he sold dope, hustled the girls, and did a lot of dirty work for people around the casinos. She said some old dude with a pile of money was involved somehow."

"Any name?"

"No."

"What else?"

"For some reason Glenda was the Jamaican's right hand. At first she did some hooking, but she moved up quickly. In the end, she said she mostly drove him around and he used her as a second set of eyes. That's how she knew he had buried some girls on the beach under the boardwalk."

"Buried, where?"

"Not too far from the safe house, under the place on the boardwalk where Wash Tub Wanda does her act."

"Wash Tub Wanda? You mean the woman who beats on the plastic dishpans with drumsticks and asks for money?"

"That's her. Glenda said the girls were buried near Wanda's spot."

Joe was riveted to Jeff's account. "Did she describe any of the girls? Did she give any details about them?" He hoped for a lead on Jessie Collier.

"No, but she said she knew how many and where, and that one of the gang that ran with them was still in a freezer."

"A freezer?"

"Yeah. In that safe house – where Klepp got killed."

"Are you sure? There's been no news about it. The police who interrogated me never said anyone else was found inside – just Klepp, Vale, and Glenda."

"All I know is what she told me." Jeff's voice and demeanor showed surprising confidence.

Joe sensed that Jeff was a misdirected loner who went the way of stronger influences. *He's honest and honestly trying to find a way out to start over,* thought Joe.

"Jeff, why didn't you come clean with all this and tell it to the cops – just like you did now to me?'

Jeff squirmed and fidgeted. "Tell the cops? I can't do that. I'm in the middle. I told Klepp about Glenda going to the safe house to get money and dope and *wham*! Klepp, Glenda, and Vale are dead. I had a warrant coming out on me for some other stuff. I tried to change things, and now I'm afraid I'm a suspect."

Joe examined Jeff. The young man looked like he had

been on the run. "You don't seem very dangerous."

"It was a minor thing. I flunked my piss test. It gets sticky because I was on probation for selling a baggie of weed. "

"You a musician?"

"No. I can't play anything or sing a note. I just love music."

"Been there."

"I haven't been home since all this happened. I've been backing into parking spots to hide my tag, eating on the run, and sleeping here in the truck."

"You look it."

"I'm scared. Listen, Joe – a cop was working with the Rasta dude. Glenda told me that more than once. And whoever it was – had once been Detective Klepp's partner."

"Yes, it was Vale, the other cop that was killed."

"No – no – *in addition* to Vale."

"Are you sure?'

"Yes. Glenda told me how the partner knew all about Vale and was high up – on both sides of the fence. She rattled on and on about how she was involved in everything. That's why I don't trust the cops. Joe, I trust you. You're the only person I can trust."

"Why me?"

"When I called – that night – I believed what you told me about one guy's actions meaning something. You talked to me like I was a real person."

"Well, Jeff, you are."

"Thanks. I knew you'd understand. That's why I've been following you. I know I screwed up helping Glenda, but I am trying to set things straight."

"Jeff, you did right. What happened to Klepp was not your fault. The question now is, 'To set things right, are you prepared to go all the way?'"

"What do you mean?"

"For the past several days I've been in a fog, but you being here, and what you told me, has pried my mind loose." He pulled out his wallet, extracted a card and said, "We need to talk to the Coffee Man. I think that *together* we know who killed Johnny Klepp."

CHANGE OF PLAN

Erskine Detwilder scanned the Internet news article, checked its twin in the newspaper, and smiled. His less than subtle suggestion that the Vale-Klepp shooting be downplayed had been heard, and, most importantly, followed by the local media.

The company's powers-that-be had sent him to Atlantic City to prepare their holdings for the next act: a transition from gambling mecca to that of a family-friendly entertainment destination. The last thing he wanted was a police scandal. The rash of crimes: the shootings, the kidnapping, and all the rest had to be quelled.

Time to pressure Coyle to wrap things up and then wrap him up, too. I'll convince him that it's in his best interest to sacrifice any assets he's been protecting, and then I'll arrange for him to be "handled." I'll have to use an out-of-town asset. These local fools are incapable of doing anything except screw up.

He grabbed the phone and made the call. When he connected he said, "Coyle, we need to talk."

"Yes – Mister D...D...Detwilder."

"You were lucky that a distraught woman took care of those fools. In the future you won't be fortunate enough to have free help. Time to eliminate the rest."

"Eliminate? I – I – I –"

"Things are different now."

"I c...c...can't."

"You'll have to clean things up by yourself – and soon."

"B...b...but –"

"Call me when you are finished."

"B...b...b...but –"

"I said. '*When* you are *finished*!'"

WHO?

Detective Rich Kona stared at the names on the wipe board and tried to eliminate them one at a time. Jeff Malone stared at the same list with the intent of making a plausible case against one of them. The pair of investigators had found this method of competition worked well for them.

"Wilkes and Rourke aren't bright enough to participate in anything like this," exclaimed a tired Kona. "And Stern is way *too* smart. Besides, all three of them are lazy bastards."

"Being too lazy to earn legitimate money may be motivation to go bad," observed Malone.

Kona pretended to weigh two items by moving his hands up and down. "Lazy *and motivated?* Tell me, how does that work?"

"I see what you mean. I could buy it."

"So, you agree?"

"It's in line with my placing those three on the bottom of the list."

"Really? You been holding out on me?" Kona joked.

"Of course, isn't that the idea?"

"Tell me what you have."

"It's what I don't have – on those three. Asset checks, time logs, phone taps, and the ever-active rumor mill, all gave me zip."

"That leaves us with Coyle, Greene, and Clamson. They are like all the rest – people Klepp called more than once in the past month. Thank God for phone records."

"But we've been peeking at Mary Clamson's phones for a long time and have nothing. If I was a betting man, I'd say she knows about the taps."

"If so, that's one point for her as the rotten apple. What about the other two?"

"Hugh Greene is a Luddite. I'd swear he never turns his phone on. He's old school – works face-to-face. He prefers to look you in the eye."

"That's one for him as a good guy?"

"Yeah, but I'm prejudiced. I worked with him once, a long time back."

"I wasn't aware of that."

"We weren't partners or anything. I was a newbie – in that gap after graduating the academy and getting on the street. Greenie headed a task force busting johns and I was assigned to do paper work. I was only there a week or so. But, I clearly remember him as a square guy, all business, and no bull."

"Definitely a point to the good. What do you think of Coyle?"

"Like Clamson, Bill Coyle is one of Klepp's former partners, and he could be a fit for the receiving end of that final call."

"Coyle and Klepp certainly had a love-hate relationship."

"Enough love from Klepp to give an ex-partner a freebie worthy of riding on 'til retirement?"

"Maybe."

"And on the other side, maybe enough resentment and hate from Coyle to kill Klepp, Vale, and the girl?"

"That would be a huge 'Maybe.' Sure, Coyle has the where-with-all to stage what we found, but like all the others, there is no solid motive. Something doesn't fit." He pointed at the wipe board in frustration. "Why would any of them want Klepp dead?"

"Say that again."

"Say what? What do you mean?"

"Klepp – why is Klepp dead – why would they want

Klepp dead?"

"What are you trying to say?"

"Could Klepp be collateral damage? Maybe he wasn't the target."

"You think Vale was the target?"

"No. He was in on it – I'll explain later why I think so."

"That only leaves the girl."

"Bingo – we have a winner!"

"I guess it could make sense."

"Of course it does – go along with me on this: the girl was the Rasta Man's constant companion, she knew too much about his dealings for her own good, she sneaks back to Rasta Man's hideout to finance her getaway, and is bush whacked by Vale and our mystery shooter?"

"But we found no money."

"The shooter took it along with any other related evidence."

"What about Klepp?"

"He's right behind the girl and gets wacked."

"Or maybe he's an additional target."

"A multiple hit is possible."

"Then what about Vale?"

"He was expendable. The shooter used the situation as cover for getting rid of an accomplice that was no longer necessary."

"Let's say I buy that Klepp is not a target. And I agree that Vale was dirty."

"We know he was."

"Then what on earth did that girl know that could be so damned important?"

"Maybe she knew why there was a stiff in the freezer."

"Maybe – maybe not."

"Whatever it was – it got her killed." He pointed to the board. "The answer is right there – we just can't see it."

"All we need is more a little more information."

BIRDS OF A FEATHER

Jeff chewed a thumbnail and twitched like a kid waiting to see the Principal. Standing at the entrance to the Atlantic City Police Headquarters was definitely the last place he wanted to be.

"You made it sound easy," he told Joe, "but now that we're here I'm scared enough to piss my pants."

"What happened to all that trust?"

Jeff was embarrassed. "Sorry. I did six months in county and I never want to go back inside."

"Me neither. It sucks."

"You did time?"

"A little," Joe said sheepishly. "Eleven days." It was Joe's turn to be embarrassed and he blushed slightly. "It was in the Sixties."

"Yeah, the Sixties, a cool time, right?"

"Not in jail. Eleven days may not compare to your one hundred and eighty, but it was the eleven worst days of my life. Hard bunks, lousy food, idiot cellmates; fifty guys in a huge open bay, and nothing but noise – no music just noise – day-in and day-out. You'll agree, anyone who has experienced it knows how much jail sucks."

Reminded of jail, Jeff visibly slumped. "I was and am so terrified of being sent back. Now look at the mess I'm in."

Joe placed a hand of reassurance on Jeff's shoulder. "Don't worry. I didn't bring you here to let that happen. You're not going back."

"I hope so." He mustered a thin smile and said, "Maybe two guys can do twice as much good."

Joe pulled out Rich Kona's card and looked at it again. "You bet! We have important information to share – more than enough to keep you out of jail, if we play it right."

"How do we play it?"

"I've found that when all else fails – try honesty. We go in, sit down, and tell them in the Internal Affairs unit everything we know."

"Internal Affairs – aren't they cops for the cops?"

"Yes they are."

"Why them?"

"They interviewed me the night Johnny died – he was working for them."

"Klepp was investigating other cops?"

"It looks that way."

"So, our plan is to work with Internal Affairs because they need us?"

"Jeff, you're way too smart to go to jail."

THE TALE

On the front end of the interview Rich Kona kept silent, allowing Malone to question, guide, and probe. Kona observed, listened, and absorbed the facts, paying close attention to what he heard.

Cases solve themselves, they always do. All it takes is patience. Sooner or later the key pieces of the puzzle appear and everything falls into place. I just need to be patient and see where this goes.

Joe continued, "I'd swear that Detective Clamson was wearing Jessie's jewelry. The woman at the consignment shop had it and she took it to Zebo's. That's certain. She must have given it to one of those thugs inside and they gave it to Clamson. When you tie it to what Jeff told you about Glenda describing how Rasta Man worked with one of Klepp's former partners it all fits. Clamson is in with the Rasta Man, his gangster bosses, and whoever was using the young girls in and around the casinos." Joe finished.

"So, why do you think there's a wider organization?"

"Klepp thought so."

"But why are *you* certain?" asked Malone

Joe answered without hesitation, "Klepp said everything was connected and that whatever Glenda would lead him to would be big. Glenda was the key and Klepp got killed because if he nabbed her he would have been able to connect Clamson directly to what Glenda had witnessed. The Mermaid necklace ties Clamson to Jessie, Glenda, and the Rasta Man. Her having the jewelry proves it. All you have to do is get the necklace and arrest Clamson. I'll testify, along with my niece, Jessie's friend, Brooke. Then you can pressure Clamson to reveal where the bodies are buried – for real." He looked to Malone, to

Kona, and then back to Malone. "It's that simple, right?"

Kona signaled to Malone that it was time for him to take over. He said, "No. It's never that simple."

Joe and Jeff both looked slightly baffled. "What do you mean?" asked Joe.

Kona continued. "The kid's story is solid. We held back some crucial information, and his knowing about the girl stuffed in the freezer clinches it with me. He's good."

Jeff smiled.

Kona continued. "Between what the two of you shared we've got a decent picture of what happened and who is involved. You've filled in a lot of the gaps in several ongoing investigations."

Now Joe smiled. "So you can move ahead and arrest Mary Clamson," he said.

"No," Kona replied.

"I'm lost," Joe said.

"It's complicated. Let me explain." Kona took a deep breath. "It's an issue of credibility." He pointed to Jeff. "His record soils him as a witness. No judge will issue search warrants and subpoenas based on his testimony alone."

Joe said, "There's mine, too."

"It helps, but in the end, it's only words. We need something *solid*."

"The mermaid jewelry should do it," Joe insisted.

"It would. But you just can't make a warrant appear out of thin air to search the home of a highly decorated career police officer, a captain no less."

"If you had something as solid as the jewelry would you act?"

"Yes, solid evidence like that would be hard for her to explain. But, like I said, I can't raid her home."

Joe got up, started for the door, and motioned for Jeff to follow. "Then it's time for us to go. I've got an idea that needs attention."

Jeff, confused and apprehensive about his status, mumbled, "But – I'm – what about my –"

"Go on," Kona told him. "We'll pretend we never saw you. If he's going after what I think he's thinking about – he'll need your help."

It did not take long for Kona's words to sink in. Jeff scampered after Joe and in seconds they were both out of sight.

Malone chuckled and said, "Rich, I do believe that you are the devil himself."

"Me?"

"Don't act innocent. You played them."

"Okay, I'm guilty. But, people have been dropping like flies and we're no closer to wrapping anything up. What would you have me do?"

"I don't know, maybe nothing. Maybe I'd have done the same as you. I just hope they don't get killed doing on their own what we can't do."

RENOVATIONS

*J*oe's really got the detective bug, Brooke told herself. *Since the funeral he's totally forgotten about me. For him the jewelry is key to understanding everything. Especially for learning what happened to his cop friend. I'm glad I was able to dodge that fat cop seeing me. I'm even gladder to know he's gone for good.*

She was on her way to the marina.

While he's occupied with that loser Jeff, I've been left alone.

She smiled.

Go ahead and do your thing, Mister Jersey Shore Joe. It's fine with me. I've got things to do and people to see. I'll worry about my jewelry later.

Brooke backed-up Joe's truck and parked it as close to the boat as possible and got out. She then searched the bed for some tools and made her way up the ladder and into the boat's cockpit. In minutes she was below deck sizing up her task.

I'll have the counter tops removed in a jiffy. The ones in the galley and the salon are no big deal. The little one in the head is trickier. Not much room to get leverage. I guess I'll have to whack it out of there. I hope no one hears me. Maybe a lot of small taps is better. It might increase my work time a bit, but even at that, I should be done in less than two hours.

She grabbed a pair of gloves, donned earphones, selected some favorite tunes, and got to work. In an hour and twenty minutes her work was done.

I'll just load up the truck, zip on out of here, and get on with business.

BREAK-IN

Jeff parked a block away from Mary Clamson's residence and looked at Joe in disbelief. "What you're saying makes absolutely no sense. We just can't break into a cop's condo."

"Not we – me," answered Joe to correct his companion. "You just did the driving."

"Great! Like that will be enough to clear me if we get caught."

"It's not if, it's when."

"What?"

"I want to get caught."

"Let me get this straight – you *want* to get caught?"

"Yes. What we say cannot be ignored if I'm caught *with the proof*. I'm going to force an investigation of Mary Clamson by breaking in and getting my hands on that jewelry."

"Joe, you are crazy."

"Maybe, but I wasn't lying when I told you one man can make a difference. Right now, I can be *that* man."

"I'm with you, Joe."

"No you're not. Just do as I told you to. Get clear of this neighborhood and call in an anonymous tip for a break-in. Just give me five minutes to get inside."

"Are you sure?"

"I better be."

"And you said jail is no place to be."

"If I am successful, I won't end up there. And, we'll catch Johnny Klepp's killer."

"This is crazy, just crazy."

"I know." He got out. "Here's hoping that Kona and Malone cover me. I am about to commit one crazy-ass crime."

SURPRISE!

Mary Clamson thought she heard the door being jimmied. *I can't believe this,* she thought. *It's broad daylight and some idiot is breaking in!*

She moved quickly and quietly from the bedroom's main area into an adjacent dressing room and closet where she kept her guns. *Whoever it is – they're in for a surprise!* She grabbed a revolver, peered through the louvers of the closet door, and watched in amazement as the intruder entered the room and made a beeline for the jewelry tree atop her dressing table.

Jesus! It's Jersey Shore Joe. What the hell is he doing here? She thought when she recognized the burglar. Joe eyed the item that was his goal and grabbed. Mary pushed the door open and shouted, "Freeze!"

Joe did just as he was told.

"This isn't a social call. Care to explain why you are here?' she asked.

Joe held up the mermaid necklace. "I came for this."

"Why?"

"It ties you to Jessie."

"Jessie? Jessie who?"

"Collier – Jessie Collier."

"I've never heard of her."

"You can claim not to know the name, but you know her. And you know what happened to her."

"What the hell are you talking about?"

"The girl – she gave you up."

"What girl? What are talking about?"

"Glenda. She told Jeff everything about you and the Rasta Man."

"Jeff? Now, who the hell is he?"

"Jeff is the guy who helped me connect all the dots. You failed to ask about the Rasta Man because you know him – all too well."

"You're not making any sense. That spill you took is making you act crazy."

"I wish I was. I really wish I was." He fingered the necklace. "But this little item proves I'm not. It belonged to one of the girls you and the phony Jamaican disposed of."

Her eyes lit up with recognition of what he was saying. She protested, "It was gift – I got it as a gift."

"Maybe so – but it's hers none-the-less – and you have it. How are you going to explain having a dead girl's necklace when they arrive?"

"They? Arrive? Who's going to arrive?"

"Internal Affairs. I had Jeff call them."

"Jeff, again? Internal Affairs?"

"Yes. I've planned this. They will want to talk about the necklace. "

She shook her head and motioned for Joe to hand her the jewelry. "Toss it on the bed – and put your hands up – all the way up."

"It won't do you any good to hide it."

"I'll be the judge of that," Mary said and tugged her blouse. Two buttons popped and fell to the floor. Joe looked at her with puzzlement. She grinned and fired directly at his chest. Excruciating pain swept through him and he collapsed.

Before losing consciousness Joe heard the call she made to 911:

"This is Captain Mary Clamson, Atlantic City Police. I am reporting a shooting. I've shot and killed an attempted rapist. He gave me no choice. He gave me absolutely no choice....I had to take him down."

JOB OVER

Erskine Detwilder tossed two slim manila folders into his briefcase, closed the lid, and took one long last look at the workspace behind the desk. "Mission accomplished," he said aloud, "time to go."

He made for the door, opened it, and began to step out.

The phone on the secured line rang.

"Who could that be?" he muttered and returned to the desk. Seeing the displayed number he added, "Crap! Not the old man – not now. I'll miss my plane." He picked up the phone.

"Detwilder?"

"Yes, sir."

"Do you have a minute?"

"Yes sir – of course."

"I just wanted to chat a bit."

"Yes sir." There was silence. After an awkward amount of time Detwilder asked, "Sir – are you there?"

"Uh – hum. Yes."

More silence.

Finally the voice said, "I had hoped you would close things down without the type of activity I've have seen of late. I think I need to make a change. "

Detwilder pleaded, "Let me wrap things up."

Silence, again.

Detwilder finally spoke, "Sir, please. I can explain."

"There will be no need of that."

The line went dead.

Detwilder attempted to reconnect. There was no dial tone. "Shit – shit – shit – SHIT!" he yelled while pounding the phone's receiver against its cradle.

From the open door behind him he heard someone. "D...d...did the b...b...business model c...c...change?"

Detwilder spun around to confront his unexpected visitor. "Coyle!" he yelled.

"S...s...surprised to see me?"

"Yes. No. I mean – no!" He stared at Coyle's hands. One was empty; one held an air gun; both wore rubber gloves. "Aw – no – no –" Detwilder whined.

Coyle grinned, said, "S...s...sorry!" and fired twice.

Two projectiles hit Detwilder's chest. Before he could fully raise his hand to the impact sites, the darts' contents took effect.

Detwilder fell paralyzed, landing on his face.

Coyle crossed the room and nudged Detwilder with one foot. There was no movement. Coyle left the room.

Detwilder lay on the floor and watched silently as the wheels of a cart approached. It was pushed by Coyle; he was alone. Detwilder could not feel his limbs being folded and bent. He could not resist being moved.

"You're heavier t...t...than I t...t...thought," wheezed Coyle as he struggled to lift Detwilder. "I know you c...c...can hear me." Coyle said.

Detwilder's field of vision swept up, left, right, and then down again as he was placed in the container on the cart. His sight was severely limited when his face was crammed into a darkened corner of the large plastic tub.

Coyle's stutter intensified as he explained, "You c...c...called the wrong g...g...guy to...to d...do a hit on me. He owed me – t...t...told me t...t...the t...t...truth. I c...called your b...b...boss." Coyle laughed. "Your b...b...boss, said, I can have the lost shipment if I close things out. He said, 'p...p...people d...disap...p...ear.'" He continued laughing and closed the lid.

Detwilder tried to scream, but no sound came from his mouth.

TUNNEL TO NOWHERE

Joe struggled to open his eyes. He sniffed sterile air. His chest ached terribly.

This is not what I've been led to expect. No white light. No tunnel. No spirit guides. Where are the spirit guides, the angels that everyone talks about?

Weakly, he called out. "Hello?"

There was no answer.

Joe was terribly disappointed.

If it hurts, you aren't dead, he told himself.

He surveyed the room, its equipment, and the oversized window allowing staff to look in. *It's a hospital. I'm in a hospital's critical care unit. I'm not dead – I'm definitely not dead.*

Joe tried to lift himself up to get a better view of his surroundings. He was unable to get very far. Tempered steel prevented him from moving very far; police issued handcuffs secured his wrists to the bed rail.

"Hello!" he called out as loud as he could. His chest ached terribly.

An attractive silver-haired nurse, a bit younger than Joe, entered the room. Joe tried to rise up again.

"Please, be still," the nurse ordered. "You don't want to wiggle that chest tube loose."

The pain in his chest increased. "Oh, man," he moaned.

"I told you not to move about."

"Sorry, Nurse uh...uh..."

The nurse's demeanor softened. "I'm Kaye. I've been taking care of you. Well, half the time I've been here. Jennie has been on the day shift."

Before Joe could respond another pang careened

215

through his chest and he flinched.

Here, take this." She handed him an injector and instructed, "It's for the pain. You can administer three small doses in a ten-minute stretch. I'd go real slowly on it, if I were you."

'Thanks. I'm –"

"Joe," she finished for him. "You're Jersey Shore Joe. Everyone in Atlantic City knows you." She nodded at the handcuffs.

Joe tugged on the cuffs. "It's not what you think. I –"

"Shush." She smiled. "I'm a nurse, not a cop."

Pain stabbed at Joe again and he thumbed the device. In a few seconds relief came and he sighed, "Wow."

"You okay?" asked Kaye.

"Super. Never been better." He hit the injector.

"Now, remember to take it easy with that stuff."

"I'll be good."

"You better be – I'm a fan." She winked and reached for the room's intercom and pressed the call button. Joe wanted to engage Kaye in conversation but she made it apparent that she was about to depart. "Now that you are awake, I can let the real cops in to see you. They've just arrived."

Kaye opened the door, leaned out, and motioned to someone out of Joe's line of sight, waved goodbye to Joe, and slipped out the door. Joe leaned forward to get a better look just as Rich Kona and Jeff Malone entered.

"Hello, Joe," Kona said for the two police officers.

Malone came toward the bed, reached into his jacket pocket, and produced a key for the handcuffs. "I wanted to take the cuffs off sooner, but Agent Kona is a stickler for details. The ballistics report only came in a short time ago."

"Ballistics report?" asked Joe.

"You heard six shots," said Malone. "But only four

bullets were found. That was the rub."

"Boom, boom, bang, bang, boom, boom." Joe let the beat out of his head.

"Right. Two loud shots, two softer ones, and then followed by two more loud ones. The first two shots – boom, boom – took out the girl and Klepp. She dropped backward and caused Klepp, who was a step behind her, to stumble down the stairs. He died in front of you without firing a shot."

"Then two bangs."

"They took out Vale. The gun, a plant, was placed in the girl's hand to make it look like a shootout went down."

"Vale didn't shoot the girl and Johnny?"

"No. The second set of loud shots –"

"Boom, boom, again."

"They came from Vale's piece. But no rounds were found. They went out a window – aimed at the ocean – to make us believe that Vale killed the girl and Klepp. Vale was tagged by the planted piece after Klepp and the girl went down. Vale's accomplice –"

"Accomplice?" interrupted Joe.

"Yeah. We figured, just like you, that one of Klepp's old partners was there. He called someone before. We figured it out when the two shots in the girl and Klepp did not match Vale's gun."

Joe said, "I was trailing the jewelry, so I'm a little confused."

"Don't be. The slug they took out of you cleared up everything."

"So, it's in the ballistics report, right?"

"Yes, the slug in you matches with the two we found in Klepp and the girl. We just gave Mary Clamson the bad news and placed her in custody. Like I said, the bullet in you proves she killed Klepp, Vale, and the girl. She damned near got you, too."

Malone unlocked the cuffs and stepped back.

Joe silently stared at the two men. After a long pause Kona broke the silence, saying, "Okay, we're done here," and left the room.

Malone stayed. "I'm sorry, Joe," Malone said. "He's a Fed and out ranked me on this case. I didn't agree with him. But, it was his call."

"Call, what call?" asked Joe.

Malone looked down. "We knew, or at least suspected, that you'd go after Clamson. We believed that the extra shots you told us about came from her gun. You were our way of proving it."

"You knew what I was going to do?"

"Yeah. You were fixed on the jewelry....and we were suspicious of Clamson. "

"So, you wanted me to get shot?"

"Not exactly." The two cops exchanged guilty looks. "We were hoping she would miss. We wanted it as the best possibility, and –"

"POSSIBILITY!" Joe shrieked to interrupt. A wave of pain shot through his chest and Joe jabbed the injector several times before he laid back, exhausted. "Jesus," he moaned. "It was just a friggin' possibility to you?"

"Yeah – but – but –"

Joe moaned, "Ohhhhhh!"

"You, okay?"

"Sure, sure," wheezed Joe. Between gasps he asked, "If you thought...she was the killer...why didn't you just test her gun?"

"Kona told you it doesn't work that way. Remember?"

"Screw the way it works!"

"Joe, you have to see it our way. We're good at figuring things out, but we can't go around grabbing guns and testing them without something more solid than just conjecture. That goes double if the gun in question belongs to a highly decorated police captain. You looking for that jewelry was a happy coincidence for us."

"So, you *encouraged* me to act on my own."

"Like I said, it was Kona's call."

"But I could have been killed."

"If you had been, we'd still have matched the bullets."

Joe tried to get up and failed when a wave of pain consumed him. "Jesus!" he cried as he jabbed the injector.

Kaye hurriedly entered the room and said to Joe, "I told you to take it easy with that."

Joe tried to jab the injector again, but his limit had been reached. "Time to go," she ordered Malone. "He's really stressing out."

"With good reason," Malone replied. "He took one for the team."

"Really? Is that what you call it?"

"Oh yeah, he's a hero." Malone patted Joe's free hand and then headed for the door. "Rest up, Joe. After we grill Clamson, we'll come back to fill you in on what you accomplished by catching that slug for us."

THE SCORE

Brooke spread a large piece of canvas over the scrapped counters lying in the truck bed. She tied the canvas down tight around them, hopped into the truck's cab, and drove west from the marina. Her destination was the U-Stor-It in Egg Harbor.

After I stash these counters and take the truck back to the Inn, I'm headed out of here for good.

She eyed her cargo in the rearview mirror and ran some numbers through her head.

Let me see – three pieces of counter with a total estimated weight of two hundred and fifty pounds – that's more than a hundred kilos. The lacquered covering can't weigh more than twenty pounds, total. Subtract that and call it an even hundred kilos. Damn – at the going rate that has to be at least fifteen million dollars of black tar heroin – and it's sitting in the bed of this worthless beater! It's amazing. After all those years in the entertainment business, Jersey Shore Joe, the musical icon of the region has been riding around in this piece of crap pick-up. I can't believe how easily people pushed him around and used him. He's a perfect example that you can't live on memories of the good old days. Broke and old is a terrible way to end up. What a loser!

She looked again in the mirror and smiled back at herself.

That's not going to happen to me. There will be no living hand-to-mouth in my future.

Half an hour later, Brooke unloaded her treasure and secured the storage locker with new double locks. On her way back to the Inn she disregarded the New Jersey law prohibiting cell phone usage while driving and called a friend.

"Sugar Daddy," she said with a laugh, "your favorite baby girl has done her part. I'll be there in a couple of hours."

"G...g...good! S...s...see you s...soon."

FLIRTING

"**Y**ou're not such a dangerous desperado after all," kidded Kaye as she wiped shave cream off Joe's chin. "I don't normally provide this level of care. Especially for a patient healing fast and able to fend for himself."

"Then why do you do it?" Joe asked.

"I'm a fan...and...it's your whiskey voice that does it."

"Is that all?"

"Not enough?"

"I'll take it," Joe said as he placed a hand behind her waist and tried to draw her close.

Kaye slid away. "Stop it, Joe. I said, hands off until you are out of here. You can woo me on the Boardwalk after you are discharged. "

"Discharged? If I'm healed, like you say, then why haven't they let me go?"

"Rumors say it will be soon."

"Rumors – all I have is rumors. No TV, no papers, no visitors. Malone said he'd come back and hasn't and I'm still waiting to find out what's going on. All I know is that I caught a bullet that caught a killer."

"Making you a hero as well as a music legend."

"That's not important."

"No? What is?"

"Understanding what *really* happened. I need to know all the facts in this muddled affair. You say I am a hero. Remember, it wasn't that long ago that I was handcuffed to the bed. I'd like to know why the quiet life I was chasing fell apart. And I still want to find the girl whose disappearance got me into all this.

"From what you've shared, the lost girl has taken backseat to other people and events."

"She got me into this mess and I think she is still the key."

"You're wrong."

"What do you mean, I'm wrong? How can a hero *and* a legend be wrong?"

"It wasn't the missing girl that got you into the mess, it was her friend."

THE SENTRY

Jeff watched her. *She's a looker. The sort that guys easily fall for. But I didn't like her the moment I laid eyes on her. There's something about her that wasn't right. Joe is fooled. But I don't think Marie is.*

He shifted his position in the cab of the truck and kept watching.

She yanked those counters out of the boat and drove them to Egg Harbor. Why? You don't do that for scrap. When she returned Joe's truck, she lied to Marie, said she wanted to visit her old school. Marie asked me to drive Brooke to the school, but instead Brooke laid on the sweet stuff, all of it fake, and talked me into dropping her off in Somerset. She thought I'd buy her line of bull about meeting some school friend. Instead, she walked in and out of the place where I dropped her off. She must think I'm an idiot. I parked around the corner and watched her produce a set of keys, get in a parked car, and drive here to this old dude's apartment. Guys his age really fall for her crap. Explains why Joe is blind to her.

He rubbed his back.

I don't know how much more of this I can take. I can't get in the hospital to see Joe. He's cut off from everyone. Even Marie, his own family, can't see him. And those cops, Malone and Kona, they treat me like I've got the plague. I think they got what they wanted out of Joe and me.

He shifted his position again.

Damn, I'm tired. She's been holed up in there for days. The only sign of activity has been him going in and out like a crazy man. He's got to be fifty years old. What on earth is she doing with him? It can't be for money, he looks as broke as all the other cops I've run across. Something is going on and I can't figure out what it is. I wish I could talk to Joe. He makes sense out of everything. When he explains stuff to me it's like he's doing his show and I'm listening on my radio.

He watched some more.

Nothing. Absolutely nothing is happening.

Jeff yawned, eased the seat back, and drifted asleep.

PLEA DEAL

Mary Clamson knew the game. She was dirty, that was plainly evident, and talking to the police was not in her interest. She was well aware of the tactics that would be used against her. She knew that the authorities would lean on her, slant every thread of evidence, and even lie to prove their point. They had to make it look like she was a rogue, a bad apple, an anomaly that proved how good the rest of them were.

Mary's objective was to work a deal that would ease the heavy fall she was about to take. She looked to her attorney who nodded in agreement that now was the time to talk.

"Look," she told Rich Kona after her days of silence, "I'm ready to talk. But only if I get a deal."

"Deal?" said Kona. "What on earth do you think you have to deal with? We've got you cold on three murders."

"But that's not what you want."

"Really?" Kona eased back in his chair and laced his fingers together behind his neck. "You know want we want?"

"Yes, I do. I know this isn't about me."

"Go on, I'm listening."

"You're more than a drug sniffer. The second you arrived in town we all knew what you were after."

"We?" He leaned forward and asked, "Care to elaborate?"

"Only if I can get a deal."

"I can't offer much."

"You haven't heard what I have to give."

"Whatever it is, it can't cover three homicides."

"It's been done before."

"Not when two of the three are police officers."

"Who were part of the 'we' I mentioned."

"Maybe one. But, no way – definitely – not two. Klepp was working for us."

"Johnny, working for you? That's hard to believe," Clamson said.

"No harder than a decorated Captain killing her ex-partner." He frowned heavily and leaned forward to address her. "You are in deep shit, Mary. So deep, I can't see a bottom. Think about it. In the joint, as an ex-cop, you are going to drown in that shit. The female prison they will send you to is as bad as any male facility on earth." He held up his hand before Mary's attorney could voice an objection to the threat. "Stay put, counselor. Your client was about to tell me something." He stared at Mary and said, "No promises. You talk and I'll decide what it's worth. If I like what I hear, I'll talk to the legal team on my side and we'll put a bottom to your shit hole." Kona looked at her attorney. "Is that legal enough?"

"It won't do," said the attorney.

"It better," said Kona, "because it's the only deal you'll get." He looked at Mary. "Killing a member of the home team counts heavy against you. Klepp was a lot of bad things, but he was a good cop."

The attorney asked, "You're serious, right?"

"Very."

The attorney shrugged. "Okay, we take it."

"Are you crazy?" Mary spit out at her attorney.

"Don't be a fool," was the reply. "You knew that their first offer will be the only one."

"But he made no real offer."

"Yes I did, "said Kona. He softened his tone. "Mary, there's no escape. The deal is that you get no deal. If the information you provide is good, if it gets us where we need to go, you get some consideration. That's the offer."

Mary slumped. After several breaths she said, "Okay, how do we do it?"

"You tell us everything, and I mean everything. I want the total list covered: drugs, prostitution, payoffs, bribes, and links to organized crime. Everything and everybody you ever saw, heard, or even thought was involved is fair game. You're going to talk and talk and talk. And when you're done, you're going to answer more questions until you are exhausted. I want to know everything about each wrong turn you made and every creep you've known since the day you left the academy. Understand?"

"Sure. But before I go over my entire life I have to get something off my chest. It's killing me inside."

"What is it?"

"The worst of it. If I tell the worst of it first, then I can give you the rest.

"Go on."

"Shovels..." She looked down and stopped.

"Shovels? What are you talking about?"

Mary shook her head, keeping her eyes pointed down. "It's only sand. You'll just need shovels because they are buried in sand."

STONEWALL

Bill Coyle signed the documents and handed them to the head clerk at the police headquarters' human resources department.

"Is t...t...that all?" he asked.

The clerk rapidly scanned the papers and said, "Yep, they look good. That's should do it. You're done. You're officially retired."

A smile painted his face and his suddenly stutter disappeared. "Good? No, it's perfect."

The clerk did not notice his changed speech and offered a perfunctory, "Good luck."

"Thanks," answered Coyle. He shoved his copies of the documents in a folder and exited the office.

Outside, he began dumping the folder in the nearest trashcan while he reached for his smokes and lighter.

In a couple of hours I'll be a ghost. No more playing at being the plodding stutterer. With a new ID my life is going to be nothing but sun and fun. In a few weeks I'll have a new face and –

His phone rang. He shook his head, fumbled a cigarette, and reached for his phone.

Not again! That cute little bitch just doesn't understand. I have to tie up the loose ends and make everything look normal. Then I can do the deal and we disappear. If anyone looks for me I want them to assume I'm retired in the Poconos fishing, just as I've been yapping about for months.

After the fourth ring, he answered awkwardly with the phone nestled under one ear against his shoulder. "Yeah, Baby. What do you want?"

"Where are you, Daddy? I've been worried."

"Paperwork was slow, nothing to get worked up about. Hang on while I light up." He set the phone down, tossed the rest of the folder, and was lighting his cigarette when he heard his name.

"Coyle."

It was Rich Kona. Two uniformed officers were a few steps behind him. Coyle correctly sensed that two more had taken positions to his own rear. Attempting to hide his nerves he said, "Surprised to see you away from the Internal Affairs office. What brings you into the bowels of the bureaucracy?

"You," Kona replied.

"Me? You must be joking." Coyle eyed the hallway's end.

"This is no joke."

Coyle's eyes were fixed down the hall.

"Don't think about running, Coyle. I have a half-dozen more uniforms outside."

"Okay." He raised his arms slowly to expose his service piece. One of the uniforms from behind, stepped up, reached around, and took it from the holster.

"I'm sure I'll be able to sort this out. Can I walk out without the cuffs?"

"'Fraid not. You know the drill. Do I need to recite the it"

"Naw – as you said, I know the drill." Coyle placed his hands behind his back and a second uniform slipped the handcuffs on with a jerk. "Whoa!" Coyle remarked in pain. "No special care for a brother in blue?"

"Again, 'fraid not," Kona said again. "You made us all look bad, real bad."

"For what?"

"Murder One."

"Says who?"

"Clamson."

"I thought she was on leave."

"We had her on ice."

"So, she ratted me out and gave you a bunch of hooey to save her ass. Big friggin' deal."

"She gave us much more than the run-of-the-mill dirt."

"For instance?"

"For instance, she gave us you."

"I told you. I'm clean."

"Detwilder would not agree."

"Detwilder?" He looked up and away. "Never heard the name. Who's he?"

"A casino exec."

"I'm drawing a blank."

"That's funny. He's the guy you folded into a trunk and placed in storage."

Coyle flinched.

Kona continued. "You got sloppy, Coyle. You paid for the storage bin with a credit card. What the hell were you thinking?"

"Shit." He hung his head down. "I was so close."

"To what?

"The good life."

"You had the good life, you just didn't want it."

"Don't preach, man. Just take me in and let me lawyer up."

"You'll need the best. We have more than Detwilder."

"You're bluffing." Coyle grinned.

"The Crime Scene unit is at the beach," Kona said.

Coyle's grin vaporized. After a moment he said, "Okay, I'll talk. I want a deal."

"No way. One songbird is all I need."

"Clamson made a deal, so I can't. Right?"

"We have more than enough."

"Then let's get this over."

Two uniforms stepped forward. One took Coyle's left arm, the other took the right.

"Grab his phone," ordered Kona.

Uniform One complied. "I think it's active," he said, handing it over.

Kona put it to his ear. "It's not dead." He pulled out his own phone and called Malone as he worked Coyle's phone. To Malone he said, "Tell me who has this number, and where they are. I want you to pull out all the stops." He recited the source of Coyle's final incoming call. "Get on it right away. I don't want any loose ends."

"Lost something?" chided Coyle.

"That's funny, Coyle, real funny. You won't be joking around when you realize you are facing life plus enough add-ons to keep you locked up until the sun burns out."

MISTAKE IN IDENTITY

Brooke tried to look casual. *This phone is hot. Thank God the line was open and I heard it all. He's been arrested. Now I'm on my own. Getting out of that apartment was smart.*

She taped a key to her phone, tossed it in the dumpster, and walked toward the end of the alley. Her plan was to hit the street, turn right, and keep going.

Everything linked to Coyle is radioactive. Thank God I used my own site to stash the stuff.

She fingered the second key to the storage locker and smiled.

I'm in possession of a fortune in dope and have to get everyone off my trail. I've thought this through and I hope it works.

She looked around, saw no one, and walked south toward the street.

I need to disappear again. I need time and a safe place to figure things out.

To the north, Jeff Breen stepped from behind a garage. *I need to see whatever it is that she tossed away,* he told himself. *She's up to no good.* He sprinted to the dumpster, saw the phone with something taped to it, and reached in. *Got it!*

Jeff examined his find.

Her phone and a key. When she bolted from that apartment she was looking terribly upset. It's a miracle I've been able to stay with her. She's on the run and moving fast. I've got to stay with her.

Before he could make a move to follow, he heard a shout.

"Don't move!" yelled a cop.

A second one approached at a full run and yelled, "Hand over your phone!"

Not realizing that the command was about the phone he had retrieved from the trash, Jeff reached into his pocket for his own. As he brought his hand out of his pocket, the cop running toward him yelled, "Don't do it!"

"Gun!" yelled the other.

It was over in an instant.

Two shots hit Jeff as his arm swung upward. He fell forward clutching a phone in each hand.

"Shit!" cried out the nearest cop. "He's unarmed."

"Oh, my God," moaned the shooter. "What are we gonna do?"

Jeff stared at the sky. A gull drifted slowly above him on a slim current of beach air. White clouds framed the bird within a blue background. His chest was on fire. He could not breathe. He faintly heard the shooter cop yell, "Call an ambulance!"

Jeff closed his eyes and did not hear the second cop's reply. "Too late. He's gone."

South, at the entrance to the alley, Brooke surveyed the scene from behind a line of shrubs.

That phone had to be hotter than hot. Those cops didn't wait one second in closing in on whoever had it in their possession. It was a miracle that idiot followed me. Him taking the blame buys me time and a clean getaway. I need to disappear. I really need to disappear.

ANOTHER TALE

Joe awoke and immediately sensed a change in his surroundings. He looked about the room, and although everything seemed the same as when he had drifted off to sleep, something was not right.

"Kaye?" he called through the intercom.

"She's not here, Mr. Kontos," a new voice said. "I'm Karen. I'll be right in."

Momentarily, the woman with the new voice appeared.

"Where's Kaye?" asked Joe.

"I can't say, Mr. Kontos. I've just come on duty."

"Do you know when she'll be back?"

"I can't...I mean...." She looked about as if she were being watched. "I'm not supposed to talk."

"What do you mean by, 'not supposed to'?"

Karen looked around again.

"You've been in protective isolation...and...and..." She scanned the room. "You've been off limits to the rest of the hospital."

"Meaning?"

"Meaning, special nurses – like her."

"Kaye?"

"Yes. Nurse Baine is not part of the hospital's regular staff."

"What you mean is that she works for the police?"

"Something like that. I've seen her before, special cases, always with the police, usually the ones from out of town."

Joe's heart deflated. *Was I just being watched?* He looked at Kaye's replacement and asked, "So why are you here?"

"Your status was changed. I think you are going home soon."

A small sense of relief crept across Joe. He closed his eyes and saw Marie, Brooke, and the Inn. "Home," he said. "I almost forgot that now I have a home to go to."

Before he could ask more about his release, the door opened. Malone entered with a smile. Kona just entered.

"Good Morning, Joe," said Malone.

"I thought you'd never return," said Joe. "It's been a week."

"We've been busy," Malone answered.

"Too busy to fill me in?"

"We've been *really* busy," Kona said curtly.

Joe paid no attention. "If I stopped a bullet for the team I think I deserve to know what it was actually for."

"We kept you on wraps to preserve your status."

"Status?"

"As an untainted source," said Malone.

"What the hell does 'untainted source' mean?" asked Joe.

"It doesn't matter," said Kona.

"It does to me. I'm the one who's been held captive."

"It was just a precaution. We had to be certain you were clean – totally clean," Kona said.

"Clean? I'm just a DJ and musician – a retired one at that. How could you ever be uncertain about me?" In more than four decades on the Shore I've built a see-through reputation. If I was involved in anything like the stuff you mentioned you'd have already known about me being a desperado."

Kona stepped in. "What you say is true. But right now we have some final things to still cover with you."

With a twang of defiance, Joe said, "Go ahead ask away."

"How well did you know Jeff Breen?"

"*Did*? That's past tense. What happened to him?"

"He was in possession of a cell phone and another item linked with the people you helped us bring down."

"What happened?" Joe was visibly upset. Kona's attitude was the cause.

"There was an altercation. Things did not go well."

"He's dead?"

"Yes."

"Mother of God! He was just a lost soul."

"A lost soul in possession of a key to a storage locker full of dope. We found about eighty pounds."

"I can't believe it," said Joe.

"He had a drug record," said Kona.

"It was small time stuff – weed only," said Joe. "John Klepp was going to help him out of the jam it made for him."

"Maybe so, maybe not. Did you know Breen was an item with the girl that was killed along with Klepp and his partner?"

"Yes, Jeff told me about how he tipped Klepp off about where to find her."

"Some tip. It's possible he set Klepp up, maybe you, too."

"Wait. You two owned up to that – remember? Jeff just drove me there."

Kona ignored the comment. "Tell us about your boat and Breen."

"There's nothing to tell. Once or twice he helped me and my friend Brooke with the repair work."

"So he knew the ins and outs of the boat?" asked Kona.

"Ins and outs? What do you mean?"

"He knew about the drugs on your boat."

"What drugs?"

"The stuff we found in the storage locker. He took it off the boat."

"Impossible. I know that boat better than I know music. It's been torn apart and rebuilt an inch at a time. There's absolutely no place any drugs could have been hidden onboard."

"I didn't say hidden. They were in plain sight."

"Plain sight?"

"The counter tops in the salon and galley of your boat – they were made of compressed heroin."

"Heroin!"

"The black tar variety – sealed and covered by a heavy layer of shellac. It was an ingenious smuggling scheme. Breen must have been involved all along. He befriended you as part of an effort to recover the shipment after the initial plan failed."

Joe slumped back into his pillows. "Drugs on my boat? Jeff? He seemed so...so...lost and vulnerable. I'm confused. All I wanted was to retire – just to get away."

"We checked out when and how you got the boat. I just wanted to confront you with this and see your reaction. I believe you were unaware of what was onboard."

Joe shook his head to clear it of the fantastic story that had been presented. He blinked several times and sighed, "This is too much, way too much."

"No," said Kona. "It's enough."

"Enough? What do you mean?" Joe asked.

"It's a final loose end. We got what we wanted."

"We?"

"The special task force," said Kona. Joe's blank look gave him a prompt to continue explaining. "Washington, the Governor, two Senators, the Congressional delegation, and a horde of heavy-contributing business interests created a multi-jurisdictional unit to initiate change. My assignment was to work within the local police structure. The powers up top have been leaning hard on us for results. Initially, the entire Jersey Shore was under scrutiny, but the focus was always on redirecting this city. Big changes were desired and we needed someone within the crime community to break. And Clamson was the one that broke. Your involvement was the lucky coincidence that gave us the edge."

"Some luck."

"You were the tipping point," Kona said.

"Big deal."

"Bigger than you can imagine." He leaned forward. "Let me explain. Since I almost got you killed, I'll tell you what I know, once. And after I do, I'll swear that I never did." In almost a monotone, Kona told Joe all that had transpired. When he ended Joe was the color of ash.

"I was used," murmured Joe.

"I'm sorry."

"I wish I could believe you."

"I understand, I really I do. I'm not proud of goading you into going after Clamson. I admit that it was not my best moment, but it worked."

"Still, I was used."

"You were instrumental in bringing down a monstrous network; one that encompassed drugs, bribery, prostitution, and murder. In countless ways it was eating this community alive."

"I just wanted to find a missing girl."

"Through you we found nearly two dozen that were lured or forced into the sex trade by that phony Jamaican. Luckily some were still alive. "

"Some?"

"We found six buried under the boardwalk."

"Was there any evidence of – ?"

"– Jessie Collier?"

"You remembered."

"Since you took a slug looking for her, I checked her against the ones we found – alive and dead. Your girl had a juvie record. Clamson and Klepp busted her as a kid, so we opened the sealed records."

"You can do that?"

"The pressure on us has also provided us with a tremendous amount of clout. Her record gave us enough to exclude her from the bodies we found at the beach."

"What about the jewelry? How did it get into Clamson's hands?"

"Maybe Collier sold it, or gave it away. We found a matching bracelet on one of the buried girls. It wasn't Jessie Collier. Trust me, she's still missing, and will probably remain so."

"So I failed."

"It looks that way."

"What do you think I should do now?"

"You can let it go, or keep looking. It's up to you. But I can't help, and I promise I won't be influencing you again one way or the other. That's over. My job is done." He reached into his pocket and offered the mermaid necklace and the handcuffs that had held Joe to the bed. "Here, take these. Think of them as souvenirs."

"Souvenirs? You have to be kidding."

"Joe, when you get discharged you'll find that what you know is nothing similar to what the public has been told. Maybe having these things will help you make some sense of it all."

"Kona, you're a piece of work."

"No, I'm just a piece of the puzzle doing my job.

BERRIES

never thought I'd set foot in this place again.
She jimmied the door to the garage, swung it open, and
entered. When she saw that her father's workbench was
still in place and laden with tools she grinned.

*Good. I can cut up the piece of counter I kept for
myself. I'll slice it into small pieces and weigh them a kilo
at a time. By the look of things I have about twelve.*

Her grin became a smile.

*That's at least four million, maybe more. Not what I
planned, but it's enough to create the kind of life I want.*

She gazed out the garage door and recalled where she
was located. Her mood bottomed.

God, do I hate blueberries.

Row after row of the commercial high bush variety
blueberry surrounded the small enclave of buildings that
was once a family farm.

*When they sold out to the corporate types I told my
folks I'd never come back, but it's a perfect place to use as
a hideout and get things ready. So, here I am back at in
the last spot on earth I want to be.*

She looked closer at the berry bushes surrounding her.

*They're not ready for harvest. No one will be in the
fields, the driveway is overgrown, and the house is
boarded up. I won't be noticed if I lay low in the garage.*

She unloaded the counter, a sleeping bag, and some
provisions to set up a temporary camp.

Two, maybe three days. Then it's adios, New Jersey.

Opening a pack of hair products, she said aloud, "Let's
see if blondes really do have more fun."

WASSUP?

Marie drove and Joe stared out the window. Every so often he absentmindedly stoked the jewelry held in his hand.

"Are you going to share with me what's going on?" she asked.

Joe remained silent.

In a few minutes she said, "Uncle Joe, I'm claiming family privilege. If you don't tell me what's eating at you, I'll nag you to death."

Joe snapped back to reality and apologized, "I'm sorry, Marie. My mind keeps going somewhere else."

"Maybe you should tell me about it."

"You're right." He took in a deep breath, and exhaled. "Here goes," he began. His trademark whiskey voice was calm and as clear as it could be.

"Being isolated from just about everything – you know, papers, you, the inn, Brooke, my boat, and even music – it was an experience that forced me to think like I have never done before. I didn't have anything to distract me and I've learned something about myself, something that I'm glad to know about because it is so negative."

"Negative?"

"I like to be liked. I'm easy to manipulate. I am a real sucker for praise."

"That doesn't sound so terribly bad."

"It is when you are made a fool."

"A fool? Uncle Joe, what are you talking about? You're the most –"

He interrupted and began a world-class rant. "What does anyone *really* know about Mary Clamson, John Klepp, and me? Nothing, or almost nothing. In the end it's the same. The public only knows what it's told. The events of the recent past are all fairy tales; a boatload of slanted facts, misdirection, and outright lies. I read a backlog of the newspaper, scoured the Internet, and grilled the hospital staff. Here's what I know: Mary Clamson shooting me has been peddled as a case of mistaken identity; Klepp, Vale, and the girl were shot in a run-of-the-mill drug bust; it's only back page news when two well-known thugs are executed and their killer commits suicide; and, nobody in a news organization even blinked when a casino exec was found neatly folded in a storage tub. Absolutely zip was said. Bill Coyle was in the middle of everything and he's never mentioned. Worst of all, six young girls, all in their teens, were stuffed under the boardwalk like so much trash and the story has been buried. That's almost a sick joke. Buried! No pun intended, but the reality is truly sickening. And get this, all the dirt, filth, and sleaze associated with this unprecedented string of criminal events is soft-pedaled because the powers-that-be want to turn Atlantic City into some sort of Vegas-Disney hybrid. Along the way I was used to make things happen. Clamson killed at least three people and she is sitting in an out-of-state jail cell with a new identity. Coyle is locked away forever, but no one will ever really know why. Kona said I helped bring down an evil empire – that's crap! I only helped it change clothes. I was used and deceived. If that's not being a fool, what is?"

"All I can say is wow!"

"Wow doesn't even begin to express how we've been had."

"What do you mean by 'we'?"

He looked down at the jewelry, and said, "I'll explain after I visit a nun."

NUN BETTER

Sister Juliana smiled when she saw her visitor, stepped from behind her desk to greet him as an old friend, and with uncustomary informality, gave him an un-sisterly bear hug.

"Jersey Shore Joe, welcome to the Sisters of Sorrows School!"

In all his years of performing, promoting, and being a DJ, Joe had rarely been greeted so warmly, especially by a nun. He was speechless. Being hugged by a middle-aged woman in a habit was not what he expected.

Sister Juliana laughed at her stunned guest, and said. "Of course you don't remember me."

"Re – re – remember?" sputtered Joe.

"Soapy's Bar," she giggled. "I served you an ocean of beer during the summer of '87."

"Oh my God!?" he exclaimed, looked heavenward, and then immediately apologized. "I'm sorry."

"That's okay." She crossed herself.

Joe looked at her as if she were an alien. "I can't believe it. You're *Soapy's Beer Bunny?*" he asked.

"Yes," she smiled, "I certainly *was*." She stepped back and waved her arms down and across in front of her habit clad form. "But, as you can see, I gave up on that life long ago."

"What happened?"

"You could say I had an epiphany."

"Beer Bunny to headmistress – sounds more like a miracle," he joked.

They laughed and she motioned Joe to a seating area. "You haven't changed a bit, Joe. A great sense of humor, and that voice...oh, my Lord, that voice."

Joe blushed.

"It's a gift from God himself, Joe. I just can't imagine the Shore without its music and your voice. You created the shared context of how people listen to the music of the Shore. What a gift!"

Joe blushed. "A gift? At times it's been a curse. Maybe you haven't heard. I'm no longer in the music business. I'm retired."

She became serious, pointed upward, and said, "Joe, no one retires from 'the call.' Trust me on that."

"There's plenty truth to that. Jeez, look at you – a nun!"

"And very glad to be one." Sister Juliana smiled and her seriousness melted. With concern in her voice she asked, "Joe, you're one of the last folks I would have listed as a potential visitor to my school. So, tell me, what set of events brought you here?"

Joe felt an immense sense of comfort in the presence of Sister Juliana. Perhaps it was how she asked, or maybe it was simply their shared past that coaxed him to share everything he had experienced since the night he walked away from the radio station.

He wrapped up his tale with, "...and that leads me to finally answering your question, 'why here?' I need confirmation of my belief that I've been duped." He handed a photo. "I'm right, aren't I?"

Sister Juliana looked at the photo and said, "They look so much alike, it's easy to see how you were misled." She pointed at the girl wearing the mermaid necklace. "That's Jessie. If you didn't know that she had hazel eyes and Brooke had brown, you'd believe they were identical twins. Often, they switched identities as their idea of a joke."

Joe exhaled a long slow breath.

"When Detective Kona told me the girl found with the matching bracelet was not Jessie, I suspected something like that was possible. The buried girl was most certainly the real Brooke."

"Oh no," Sister Juliana murmured. "I feared that something terrible would come of their relationship and prayed for it not to be so." Tears appeared. She reached for a tissue. "And you are here because you are going after Jessie, right?"

"Yes. Tell me about her – everything."

"She was as worldly and complex as Brooke was naïve." Sister Juliana wiped her eyes and blew her nose. "Jessie is special for me. She was my biggest challenge."

"Challenge?"

"Yes, a challenge. Jessica is that one student that tested my faith. You see, I played a large role in getting her into school and she repaid me by testing me in every way she could imagine. Please, don't get me wrong. I wasn't expecting gratitude. I did it because I could. What I did not expect was her hostility. Jessie viewed herself as an outsider. And although she reveled in the role, she blamed me for getting her family to make her attend our school"

"What was your connection to her family?"

"I knew them in Hammonton, where I grew up."

"The Blueberry Capitol."

"Yes. That's where Jessica is from, or at least near there. Her people were blueberry farmers, and when they sold their property to a corporate conglomerate they used the windfall to buy several businesses in South Jersey and to educate Jessie. I *suggested* they consider our school. Jessica came here as a freshman and immediately was a problem student."

"Was it a country mouse, city mouse sort of thing?"

"Heavens no! Jessie was welcomed with open arms. She chose the role of outcast. In her twisted mind it gave her a license for revenge on anyone whom she believed had slighted her."

"You said her mind was twisted."

"I was being kind. In reality Jessica was manipulative, cruel, cunning, and plain-old-fashioned mean. When she wanted something she got it by using intelligence and charm. Jessie was a chameleon and could control people through acting whatever part it took to advance her desires. Once she focused on something Jessie was unstoppable. And she wanted Brooke. Jessica came back to the school and recruited Brooke into her personal circle. I still hear news from friends in my past; they told me Jessie ran with a wild crowd in Atlantic City."

"How did Jessie and Brooke team up?"

"After Jessie graduated three years ago –"

"Three years? She's that much older than Brooke and can pass for her?"

"It was easy for her. Jessie is a chameleon of the highest order. Even for people who knew Brooke, it was easy to be fooled by Jessie becoming the younger girl. And Brooke went along with it by pretending to be Jessie. Brooke saw it as friendship, but it was just another piece of Jessie's manipulation puzzle. Its completion came when Brooke turned eighteen and left school. The Paxtons had gone on an ill-conceived world-trip and we here at the school had no right to stop Brooke from departing. So the pair went to Atlantic City and only God really knows what happened."

"Jessie was Jessie, and Brooke paid for it. That's why I am going to find her. She has to be held accountable for her role in Brooke's death."

"There is something more."

"More? Oh yeah – the drugs. Tracking down the drugs she stole is important."

"I meant getting even."

"Getting even?"

"Jessie was *my test*...and I'm afraid I have failed. It's a terrible sin not to forgive and I cannot forgive her."

"Then you must help me find her. All I need is a lead. If you were Jessie, where would you hide?'

"I have no idea. But I do have a good idea who would."

"Go on."

"Her brother, Stan. He manages one of the family businesses. I think he's your best lead."

"Where I can I find him?"

"Egg Harbor. He runs a U-Stor-It franchise."

HEY BRO!

Stan Collier was lured away from the pornographic images on his laptop by the sight of the man walking toward the office. Stan did not like the look of the guy from the moment he got out of his ratty truck.

"He's not a customer," muttered Stan, "and he's not a cop. But I'd bet the payroll that he's here because of her. Whenever I get this feeling I know it's because Jessica is involved. It's just so."

Stanley Collier was not a forceful personality. Small, and wispy, he was as timid as Jessie was resourceful. It was his nature to flee and never fight. Closing the store was the most aggressive thing he could think of doing.

"Hurry, hurry!" Stan urged himself. He moved quickly to the door and flipped the closed sign outward. "It's worth a try," he mumbled.

Joe saw Stan move the sign and tried the door anyway. "Open up, Stan," he shouted. "You can talk to me, or the police – take your pick!"

Stan, the wimp addicted to X-rated videos, opened the door. "I knew it," he whined. "It's because of her, right?" He did not wait for, nor need an answer.

"I had a feeling you came here because of Jessie." He moved aside to let Joe into the office of the storage facility.

Joe wasted no time on pleasantries. "Just tell me where she is."

"I don't –"

"Shut up!" ordered Joe. "I'm not in the mood to hear any more lies. Your sister told enough. I need to know where she is – NOW!"

Stan was visibly shaken. When the police had asked a lot of questions about the items in the locker he had somehow handled the strain. He had made it through. But this was different. His nerves were frazzled, and Joe was beyond aggressive.

Joe pressed again. "Tell me where Jessica is hiding!"

"I...eh... I...eh...I –" He sobbed like a frightened child.

Joe displayed no sympathy. "Jessica stored the counters here, but you let the cops think Jeff Breen rented the locker. Didn't you?"

Stan nodded between sobs.

"You let her use a second unit to store the stuff she stole, right?"

Another nod.

"Listen, Stan. You're in deep. Maybe she conned you like she did everyone else. But that might be hard to sort out with the cops. You don't look like the kind of guy that could handle what happens if they find out how you've helped her. Jail is not for you – trust me."

Stan moaned, "Ah – ah –" He wiggled and nervously stamped his feet.

"Tell me where she is, Stan!"

"Ah...ah...ah..." He stalled for time, but Joe had no patience.

"Do it!"

Stan complied. "She's at our farm."

"Where is that?"

"N – n – near Hammonton, off Nesco Road, about f – f – five miles from town."

"She better be there."

"S...s...he is."

"For your sake, I hope you're right. If she is there, and if you don't alert her – I'll forget everything I know about you and the dope that was in the second storage unit."

Stan jerked to attention, stopped shaking and stuttering, and blurted, "I won't say a thing, I promise!"

Joe gave instructions. "Draw me a map to the farm,

forget that I was here, and get on with your life – just don't tell her I'm coming. Jail will kill you, Stan. It really will."

Stan frantically searched for a pen. "I want Jessica out of my life as much as you want to find her. She's nothing but trouble. If it weren't for her I could have been –"

Joe pointed to the video still playing on the laptop. "Put a lid on it, loser. Your brain is hardwired to the wasteland."

END OF THE ROAD

Joe looked at the map one last time. *This is it*, he told himself as he eyed the lane leading to the abandoned farm. *I hope my second try at being a vigilante goes better than the first.*

He rubbed the spot where Mary Clamson's bullet had almost ended his life.

What the hell am I doing? My idea of a quiet retirement was piddling around the inn, time on the boat, and writing my memoir. Anyone in their right mind would sit back and call the cops. I'm here, but I really don't have a plan.

His feet seemed to move on their own. Soon he was at the end of the lane which led directly to the garage. *Just as I thought, she's here.*

Before he could worry again about not having a plan he heard a voice from behind say, "I never expected you to show up, Joe."

He turned to find the girl he had known as Brooke pointing a gun and sporting a blonde crew cut.

"Do you think that's necessary, Jessie?" he asked.

She laughed. "You're here, you know my name, and you've seen my new do. So, I'd say, 'yeah' I need this. At least for the time being." She waved the gun to direct Joe. "Head into the garage. We need to have a chat."

Joe did as he was told.

Inside, his eyes slowly became accustomed to the dark, and from the state of her gear and the packed drugs he surmised that Jessica was about to leave. Everything was packed and stacked next to the car ready for loading.

From behind Joe heard Jessica enter and close the door.

"Back up against the wall, Joe. And ease to your left until you meet the other wall. When you get there, stretch your arms out and place your palms against the wall with your thumbs down."

"A lonely and vulnerable young girl can't be too careful, right?" Joe quipped as he eased along the wall.

"It's not that I don't trust you. It's just that I don't trust anyone."

"Really? I'd have sworn you just don't care about anyone." He stopped when he found the corner and turned to face her.

"It's the same thing." She waved the gun. "Put your hands on the wall the way I said."

"That's not surprising – coming from you," he said as he moved his hands.

"What on earth do you know about me?" she asked as she dropped the gun a bit. "Until just recently, you only thought of me as Brooke, right?"

"That's true. But regardless of the name you used I was your friend and honestly concerned."

Her tone mellowed. "You're a nice guy and easy to like." She eased her stance. "Tell me – how'd you figure out I wasn't her?"

"The jewelry."

"My necklace?"

"No – the matching bracelet. It was found on a girl buried at the beach. When it was determined that she was not Jessica Collier my mind wouldn't let go of the potential explanations. Eventually I landed upon the possibility that you were posing as Brooke and that the girl with the bracelet was her."

"What did the cops say about your genius as an investigator?

"Nothing."

"What?"

"They don't know – at least not about your switching roles."

"Why not?"

"You might say I was embarrassed."

"Embarrassed?

"For being so easily duped."

She laughed. "I've got to admit it, you *were* easy to fool."

With a hint of both hurt and sarcasm Joe said, "Thanks. It's just what I needed to hear."

"Ahhhh – I'm sorry, Joe." She smiled, and still holding the gun on Joe, stepped closer to him. "I didn't mean to hurt you." She eased forward more. "Like I said, I grew fond of you, Joe. You're okay – for an old dude."

Joe eased his hands down a few inches.

Jessica stopped him. "Ah, ah," she warned, "keep 'em up like just I told you."

"It hurts to keep them up. You know – I was shot retrieving *your necklace.*"

"Oh – yeah, I guess I should thank you for that." She came within inches, stuck the gun in his ribs, and placed a moist kiss on his mouth.

She smelled of hair product, gun oil, sweat, and lime perfume – the kind beach girls wore. Joe felt a swirl of arousal within his core.

It would be nice, a voice from within exclaimed, and Joe's inner demon roared. He responded and kissed her back.

"Whoa, dude," she warned. "If you want to make a move on a girl, you need to give her a present. Where's my mermaid?"

"In my pocket."

She leaned in, purred, and teased, "Gee, and I thought it was you getting happy." Her tease turned to a taunt. "Pull it out, Joe. Come on – let me see what ya got."

Joe turned a deep red.

She laughed at his embarrassment. "I meant the

necklace, you old perv. Come on, if you play nice maybe we can work something out. You know – we can head up to New York and turn some heads."

Joe could not believe what he felt and heard. A small piece of him wanted it to be so, but everything that comprised the man known as Jersey Shore Joe told Joe, the Retiree, that this chameleon had changed its hue. During his rough-and-tumble life in the music and bar scene he had seen it countless times in countless variations.

I'm too smart for this ploy, so how did she fool me? He wondered. *Was I blinded by an old man's wishful thinking for one last fling? She played me. I didn't see but Marie did. It's simple as that – I didn't want to.*

"You can't be serious," he said.

"We can talk about it *after* I get my necklace."

Jessie moved closer. A wave of youthful female heat surrounded him. She tried to play him again with proximity, her scent, and the double meaning of her teasing. "Come on, Joe. I want it. Come on give it to me. Come on," she begged.

"Sure, Baby, sure," Joe played back. He reached into his pants and pulled out the object of his desire. *She's a child-like poisonous snake,* he told himself. *After she gets her toy, she'll kill me, and run with the drugs.*

She tucked the gun in her waistband and grabbed. "Oh my God – it's so much better than I remembered."

"I'm so glad you like it," Joe said as she placed the necklace around her neck.

As she made the movement, Joe reached again into his pocket.

Jessica giggled uncontrollably. "A big boy surprise?" she teased, with a pinch of mockery.

"No!" he said with a firmness that caught her off guard. Joe extracted the handcuffs Kona had given him, grabbed one of her arms, and flipped a cuff into place. Before she could react, he repeated the move on her free arm securing them behind her back.

"You bastard!" she yelled.

"It's over, Jessie," he said calmly.

"No!" she screamed.

He snatched the gun from her belt, and pushed hard, and downward.

She landed on her rear and screamed again, "You bastard, you lousy old fucking bastard!"

"I can't let you leave, especially with those drugs. And I won't be a repeat fool. With the money from the drugs you'd dump me, or worse. As soon as it would fit your needs you sacrifice me – just as you did Brooke. You've got to come clean about her."

With the mention of Brooke, Joe watched the chameleon come alive and transform once more. From her honey-dipped tongue came, "I did not have anything to do with her overdosing. Joe, you just can't believe that I would *ever* do *anything* to harm her."

"Save your act for the cops. I said nothing about Brooke overdosing. Mentioning it is your admission of guilt."

The appearance of truth prompted more honey. "Listen, Joe – I'm as much a victim as her. I –"

"Stop!"

The chameleon ignored him. She whined, "I was so alone and hurt. I was so lost. I –"

"I said, 'stop.' I don't want to hear it. You chose to run with the scum of Atlantic City. You returned to the school that nurtured you and lured Brooke to her death. There is no excuse. If you were abused, I'm sorry. If you were neglected, the same goes for that. If the big kids laughed at you, or one of them was a bully, so what. There is no excuse, and I just don't *want* to hear your lies."

THE END IS NEVER REALLY THE END

Rich Kona observed Jessie Collier through the mirrored window and told Joe, "I have seen a lot of hard cases in my time, but she's the hardest of the hard. She's good at being bad; has a new twist for each item we put before her; hops from one state of denial into another."

"She's said nothing?" asked Malone.

"On the contrary, she's said a lot. I've got a team of agents working on her and they can't keep up – even using video recorders and computers. She's alone, in a cell, and without even as much as a scrap of notepaper to keep track of the web she's spun, and she's out front of them. None of it makes sense. She's either the smartest person I've seen, or she's nuts."

"Maybe both?"

"Yes, it could be. In any event, at least we can keep her off the streets for a while."

"A while? What does that mean?"

"I'm not sure."

Malone got agitated. "I don't understand by, 'not sure.' She was in the middle of everything. We can place her on the boat with the drugs; she stored them, and set up the Breen kid. Add that to recruiting girls into prostitution and being in possession of some of the heroin – isn't that enough to send her away forever?"

"Yes and no."

"Explain it to me."

Kona pointed to the observation window. "She's weaving a good tale. You know – the one about the poor little waif lured to the big city and caught up in forces beyond her comprehension and control. It might play well before a jury. And, then there is the larger problem."

"Which is?"

"If her defense lawyer threatens to reveal any of the crap we have worked so hard to hide."

"So you think she might beat what we have?"

"The possession charge is the strongest. The rest is not so cut and dried. Due to 'other considerations,' there's nothing really solid to use."

"Then we have more work to do."

"It's not '*we*,' it's *you*. It comes from above. The task force is no longer interested in Jessica Collier. She's yours as soon as I can get my team packed to leave town."

"You're joking!" Malone's agitation spiked.

"It's no joke. I have my instructions."

"From where?"

"Higher up. The Powers That Be, as they say."

"So, what am I supposed to do with her?"

"Offer her a deal," Kona said with little emotion.

Malone's frustration gushed. "*Another* deal!"

"Take the partial victory."

"Easy for you to say."

"Look at it this way...at least it will keep her off the streets of Atlantic City, America's Newest Playground."

"What happens when she gets out?"

"By then, the shine will have faded."

"On her, or the city?"

"Probably both."

DOWN THE SHORE

Joe's life had considerably slowed. He sold the boat. And, due to his injuries, Marie had restricted him to performing only the lightest of duties at the Inn. Restless and worrisome, he spent much of his time trying to make sense of what had happened, but could not. The song in his head would not let him be. An earworm ate at his grey matter, and he had no peace.

"Unbearable torture," is how Joe described the idiotic Doo Wop tune that "Big Boy" John Klepp kept performing over and over and over in his head. Endlessly and without the slightest break Joe heard Klepp's croaky voice sing, "It ain't rocket science, Baby! All the creeps know each other! No, it ain't rocket science! They know each other! Baby! Baby! Baby!"

A stiff breeze and salt air could sometimes make the song go away and in his search for peace Joe often made his way to the boardwalk. One day, while seated two blocks from the Inn he mercifully heard, "The wind and waves make wonderful sounds, Mister Kontos, but I believe you know a great deal about some better ones."

The comment came from a frailish old man wearing an expensive silk suit and shoes definitely not made for the beach. He pointed toward the Inn and said, "The young lady at the B and B said I might find you here."

"Do I know you?" Joe asked.

"Not personally. But you did work for me once upon a time." The old man laughed.

"Me work for you? I think I'd remember that."

"Yes, you did, but we never met." He extended a frail hand. "I'm Wendell Pinkering."

Joe carefully shook the old man's hand. "That was a

265

long time ago. It was my last job."

"And it's why I am here."

"I quit."

"Yes, and with good reason. I let my son run that business and I'm afraid he made a mess of things. He should never have allowed you to slip away."

"Trust me – there was no slippage."

"Be that as it may, I have a proposal for you."

"Proposal?"

"Yes, if you are interested."

Joe gave no indication of wanting to hear what his visitor had to say. After a long moment of silence the elderly man asked, "Could I induce you to work for me again?"

"You're kidding."

"No, I'm quite serious. The one good thing my son did was to use the tape you left him. Your audio 'Goodbye Tour' received the highest ratings. I want that sound for my re-make of Atlantic City."

Joe stared out at the water. "I'm a dinosaur. My taste in music does not fit in today's world."

"But you really must come back to work for me."

"Mr. Pinkering, with all due respect, the answer is 'no'."

"Things have changed. Your music, the classic sound of the Jersey Shore, it symbolizes a time gone by, *and that is what I want*! I see Jersey Shore Joe as a centerpiece to a renewed radio presence within my revival of Atlantic City. I know that some people are fanatical fans of the music you represent and I want visitors to have that authentic Jersey Shore experience; the one that only you can produce." Pinkering reached into his pocket. "Here then, take this. If you'd like to be the Musical Director for my Jersey Shore business interests, the job is yours. I'll have an employment contract waiting." He gave Joe a business card, shook his hand, and turned to return to the Inn at a slow pace.

The card read: Wendell Pinkering, Senior, Chairman and CEO, Consolidated Entertainment International. The card's innocuous tagline screamed at him, "Your Family's Best Value for Values Based Entertainment!"

Joe looked at the card and was immediately transformed. Wheels clicked, pieces fit, and the puzzle was a puzzle no more. He knew what the old man really represented and who he was. The offer was not just about music.

Joe quickly caught up with Pinkering. "It sounds beyond ambitious, Mr. Pinkering,"

"It is. My plans for Atlantic City are proceeding on schedule and there is a role for you. In fact, I have a lot of ideas for the entire Shore – from Sandy Hook all the way down to Cape May. I even have some special ideas for improving Ocean City."

"It does not need improvement."

"Oh yes it does. The silly alcohol rules have to go and –"

"That's what makes it a family place."

"No – no. It's not in my plan – not in my plan. But details such as that are not for you to be concerned with.

"Really?"

"Oh yes – what I want you to focus upon is the return – may I say, the revival – of the Jersey Shore Sound...led, of course by none other than Jersey Shore Joe himself! What do you say? Will you work for me?"

"No."

"Money is no object!"

"I've learned that when people say that it always turns out to be the most important object."

"I want to ask you something."

The elder Pinkering stopped, turned about. He appeared very pleased that Joe had decided to continue the conversation. To Pinkering, it meant that he had hooked his man.

I have him! He thought. *Just a matter of time....and money.* For an instant he looked more like a dry lizard-like wizard than a wrinkled old man.

"Of course, Mr. Kontos, ask any question. I'm at your disposal," he said with a slight trace of smugness. "What would you like to know?"

In his trademark voice Joe asked, "Do drugs and young girls come as part of the package? Or, do I need to get Jessie Collier to do the recruiting?"

Pickering froze.

Joe stepped forward, grabbed the old man's arm, and slid his grip downward to obtain leverage. He pressed hard and leaned in close.

Pinkering stiffened and remained silent.

"Cat got your tongue?" asked Joe. He applied more pressure and guided his captive down the boardwalk. "Come on...I think we need to talk, and then maybe, well take a ride."

AN ARMY OF ONE

Marie poured Kaye Blaine a cup of coffee, did the same for herself, and took a seat at the table on the Inn's rooftop deck. "He spent a lot of time on the boards."

"The boards? You mean the Boardwalk, right?"

"Yeah – that's what we call it." She took a sip of her coffee and continued. "Uncle Joe liked to walk the boards then sit at one of his favorite spots. It was his way to process what happened. His being taken in by Brooke – I mean Jessie – it really affected him."

"He was such an earnest and solid man," Kaye said.

"That he was," Marie agreed.

"And his voice! It made him so attractive."

"I know. My circle of friends expanded dramatically after he arrived. All the women could do was talk about that distinctive voice of his."

"That voice and his love of music made him a legend – a true living legend."

"His interest in music died, you know." Marie shared sadly. "Can you imagine Jersey Shore Joe not listening to music?"

"Depression can do that," Kaye said.

"Yes, I imagine so, but at the very end – the last time I saw him – he was different. Very different."

"How so?"

"He came in from his last walk looking for the keys to his truck. He had the old man with him. It was all so odd."

"He gave no clues to what was going to happen?"

"Uncle Joe said he had a job to do. He seemed pleased, like he was elated, maybe even ecstatic. He seemed truly happy – even though I'm certain that then he knew that he wasn't coming back."

"What convinces you of that?"

"When I told him you had booked a room he really lit up – like fireworks going off inside. And then, real sad, he said, 'Tell Kaye hello...and, please – please tell her I am sorry I missed her.'"

Kaye was silent for a long time. Finally, she asked, "What else do you remember?"

"The old man, Pinkering. He was very upset. No. Looking back – I'd say he was frightened."

"Did he say anything?"

"No. He just stood there, very quietly, rubbing his arm."

"He made no attempt to leave, or call out for assistance?"

"No, he was totally under my uncle's control. But I was so unaware of what was really happening."

"And Joe, what did he do then?"

"He spoke with me – briefly. We had a very short conversation, he kissed me goodbye, and then they left."

"Pickering just went along without uttering a word?"

"Yes. They drove off in Uncle Joe's truck, leaving the old man's car behind."

"It appears that Joe was totally in control."

"Uncle Joe always was the producer and director of his show."

"And I suspect that goes for the accident, too."

"Accident? He was too good a driver for it to be an accident. Plus, he never exceeded the speed limit. Jersey Shore Joe always told audiences to 'stop to smell the roses.' His truck hit that overpass on the Garden State Parkway at well over a hundred miles-an-hour. It was no accident."

"He intended to crash?"

Marie sighed and said, "Yes."

"Are you certain?"

Marie explained, "During that last exchange he said to me, 'one good person can change everything – really.' I believe he hit that overpass on purpose. He did not want Pinkering to survive."

"Murder-suicide," Kaye declared.

"I don't think so. It was something else...something more."

"You mean as some sort of sacrifice?" Kaye wondered aloud.

"No...more like an obligation, or his duty." Marie topped off both of their cups and looked out toward the boardwalk. Laughter and joyful voices rode inland on a breeze scented with the smell of Johnson's caramel-corn as the lights on the Ferris wheel turned on. "He loved this place so much," she sighed. "I think Uncle Joe believed he was protecting his home."

Kaye agreed, "Yes...it's what a good man would do."

ABOUT THE AUTHOR

Born in Blue Island, Illinois, Del Staecker grew up in two very different worlds: The surreal artist's community of Chicago's Old Town (where the likes of Jack Kerouac, Allen Ginsberg and Bob Dylan hung out at his Uncle Erling's exotic bird shop), and the small town normalcy of Boy Scouts, Little League baseball, and working on his relatives' farms.

At fifteen Del survived leukemia and penned his own bucket list. He has been a soldier, a farmer, a teamster, lived on a boat, traveled much of the world, and completed all but one item on his list of adventures. Currently, this Life Fellow of the Royal Society of Arts and Executive Committee member of the International Association of Crime Writers lives in his Pennsylvania home, which is shared by his wife, the stories that must be told, and the colorful characters in his head. Del Staecker's crime/thrillers are fast-paced, character filled, and as addictive as M&M's.

ABSOLUTELY AMAZING eBOOKS